As Long As
She Needs Me

As Long As
She Needs Me

Nicholas Weinstock

Cliff Street Books

An Imprint of HarperCollins*Publishers*

HarperCollins books may be purchased for educational, business, or sales promotional use. For information please write: Special Markets Department, HarperCollins Publishers Inc., 10 East 53rd Street, New York, NY 10022.

FIRST EDITION

Printed on acid-free paper

Library of Congress Cataloging-in-Publication Data
Weinstock, Nicholas.
   As long as she needs me / Nicholas Weinstock.—1st ed.
      p. cm.
   ISBN 0-06-019824-9
   1. Women publishers—Fiction.   2. Administrative assistants—Fiction.   3. Weddings—Fiction.   I. Title.

PS3573.E3969 A9 2001
813'.54—dc21   00-047479

01   02   03   04   QU   10   9   8   7   6   5   4   3   2   1

for Amanda

Acknowledgments

I AM GRATEFUL to Jeanine Kemm, Stan Ades, and the multitalented Amy Veltman for their daring prenuptial spywork; to the staffs of the St. Regis Hotel, B.E. Windows on the World, Tiffany and Company, and the Idaho Division of Tourism Development for their guided tours and tutelage; to the noble Mercantile Library, my home away from home; to Bliss Broyard for her timely suggestions; and to Jennifer Belle for her incomparable smarts and friendship. I am also indebted to my editor Diane Reverand, who demonstrated great faith and famous know-how; to Matthew Guma for his hard work; to Svetlana Katz, titleist extraordinaire; and to my agent Tina Bennett, fairy godsister and friend.

Lastly, I want to thank Savannah Bee Weinstock for many staggering midnight hours of editorial reflection, and the beautiful Amanda Beesley, for much more than I can say.

O Wedding Guest! This soul hath been
Alone on a wide wide sea:
So lonely 'twas that God himself
Scarce seemèd there to be.

—Coleridge

The Ring

T O BE A PERSON'S ASSISTANT is to be, of course,
her boss. While she trumpeted the orders and
wallowed in the recognition, it was he who quietly
decided her weekday schedule and predetermined her
weekends; who owned all her secrets, orchestrated her
life. She was the Dawn of Dawn Books, commander
of a quavering staff of dozens of adults; but without
his scurrying support and whispered translations she
was nothing. She was a cracked figurehead, an

empress without clothes, to be mended and swaddled daily, as we do for the least and most powerful of our species. As he did particularly well.

He dodged a herd of tourists outside the Empire State Building and wove a path through the summer traffic. It had been months since he'd wandered the city beneath its bright blue rectangles of daylight, as it was dim at the hour he got to the office, black by the time he left. He hopped over the curb and yanked at his tie, hunching lower and closer to the bobbing heads of pedestrians. Looking harder around their feet. With luck it would still be there, undiscovered on the simmering pavement by any hunter or gatherer other than him. He would find it before she got out of her meeting. He would be back at his desk in time to photocopy her AmEx bill and chronologically order her messages, to call her limo service and confirm that there would be none of the smiley driver chitchat of last time. He checked his watch. He had thirty-four minutes. A tall order, he thought, and mustered a smile.

She would have eaten at the customary five-star landmark, as it was a Thursday lunch, walkable weather. He knew her schedule and preferences better than he knew his own. At the moment he could barely remember his own. Had he ever slept late? Gone to plays? Worn a hat? An entire imagined life sparkled before him—a mirage of four-course brunches and late-night swing dancing, of lounging about in extra-large pajamas—before the vision winked shut. He reached the darkened entrance of Le Pouvoir, swam through the air-conditioning and past the bronze columns and lemon-draped tables to her usual corner. But it wasn't there. He dropped to a knee, shoved a chair. Nothing. After double-checking with the busboys and stooping to question the maître d', he hurried back outside and downtown toward the office, eyes on the sunny blur of the sidewalk. Stomach in knots. She would have walked in the shade, it occurred to him, and he loped across the street.

And there it was, by the foot of the mailbox. Hundreds of thousands of dollars recovered. But that was a bottle cap. A circle of spit on the manhole cover. A plastic earring in the green-rimmed puddle by the curb. He dabbed his shirt against his chest and glanced again at his watch. He had been away from his desk for thirty-eight minutes. Forty-six by the time he had almost picked up a condom, inspected and tossed a Canadian coin. Fourteen, now thirteen, before she'd be out of her paperback meeting and bawling his name. Ten years of this; but that sort of counting was no help. This was fun. That was more like it. A field trip. A scavenger hunt. *Lucky me*, he reconsidered. He mouthed the words down Madison Avenue. *Lucky me, lucky me.*

At first he'd hated the job. Fresh out of college, tender to the touch of injustice, he used to name and keep track of her offenses as if compiling a case to impeach. Nailfilegate. The Cuban Memoir Crisis. Unnamable was the time she'd had him FedEx her tropical fish, unforgettable the day she took up fencing. His official duty was to keep track of her statistics and deadlines, to keep her authors and employees and neuroses at bay; yet his chores went well beyond that. Between runs to her dry cleaner and re-reorganizations of her files, he pored through all her submissions and edited every one of her books. In tense meetings with top executives she crushed budget proposals and title ideas with sneering condescension; but thought e-mail was a gender until he had explained it, and tried to speak aloud to an ATM machine before he hushed her and showed her how to work it. Dawn needed him—desperately, confidentially—and it was this need that had kept him tied to his post all these years. Who else got the chance to be needed like that? Who else had shopped for her deodorant, met her ophthalmologist, seen her cry? Contrary to company-wide opinion, he was not enslaved by her famous outbursts but rather moved by them, and therefore unmoved. He had become dependent on her reliance on him. Having spent so long at her side, under her thumb, he couldn't budge.

He had gone into book publishing for the usual reason, the silliest of reasons: for books. As a college English major—scanner of verse, skimmer of classics—he had vowed to aid in the creation of works of art while his fellow graduates manufactured meaningless dividends and portfolios. Underpaid by the company and overwhelmed by the mystique, he had set out to toil in the diamond mine of literature: to unearth treasures and hand them over, to limp home empty-handed but lit and warmed by their glow. He was flagging by the end of the first year, dead broke by the start of the third. The mine was airless and wracked by explosions as its workers scrabbled to find something pure.

Yet it no longer pained him, he thought as he walked. He had grown stronger by now, or else weaker; numb to the paper cuts at his dignity, the stapled holes in his self-esteem. Plus the job kept him busy. Single people needed to keep busy. Not to mention the fresh air and exercise *(this* —he breathed deep —*is fresh air and exercise)* whenever she misplaced an item outdoors. He read books for a living: what could be better than that? But he didn't read books; he only oversaw, or undersaw, the niggling details of their mass production. Although he had been promoted when necessary over the years, the elevation was strictly semantic: from assistant to editorial assistant to assistant editor without a change in rank or location. Most recently, and rhetorically, he'd been appointed executive editorial assistant to the editor in chief. A gatekeeper, a rainmaker. A fishmailer. There had been no party to mark the tenth anniversary of his servitude, and the omission that previous Tuesday had come as no surprise. Higher-ups got cake in the conference room, company paperweights as brassy tokens of respect. Assistants got to gather the smudged napkins and pick crumbs from the chairs, lighting and blowing out the notion that they had a good job and were good at it.

He kicked aside a spread-eagled newspaper. Rocked a steel trash bin back and forth. He was short of breath, empty-handed, with time running out. How the hell did one lose something like that? She had to have dropped it on purpose, hurled it at the climax of yet another fight with you-know-who. It must have glittered, airborne, before plinking and rolling somewhere nearby. *Somewhere between goddamn lunch and the goddamn office—you tell me*, she had instructed as she strode into her meeting and ordered him out.

That was fifty-two minutes ago.

And that—a flicker by the hydrant—was it.

Crouching down, panting lightly, Oscar lifted the ring. Lucky her. Diamonds gleamed the length of the band, chips and boulders of light, sparking rainbows on his palm as he turned it over and over. The woman had taste; or rather, you-know-who did. It had the fiery looks of an engagement ring—but not in this case. Never for Dawn. You-know-who would come and go like her other you-know-whos, vanish like all the dates with divorcés he'd had to arrange and confirm over the years, the vacations with wheezy golf writers and weekends with boozy media moguls that he'd had to schedule and cover up. Such ungainly side-steps would be the dance of Dawn's life; and he was her permanent dance partner, handling her as she stomped. They were stuck with each other, left to each other by default. Husbandless and wifeless. Raging boss and aging assistant. Until death did them part.

Oscar was back at the doors of the publishing house with two and a half minutes to spare. He turned, fist closed in his pocket, to look over the frantic population of Midtown: over all the men and women heading toward each other, just missing each other, moving along. *We are hunting a ring*, he thought, *every one of us, without directions.* He closed his eyes to the clashing symphony of life in New York, the horns and percussion of people not quite getting what they want. The faint refrain of the same old question.

How could a city crammed with so many millions of people remain, for so many of them, precisely one person short?

The Proposal

THE PITY OF modern romance lies in the depths to
which one sinks in an effort to fall in love. The
groping buffoonery of singles bars. The long-shot
quiz shows that we call blind dates. Self-respecting
individuals find themselves scrawling personal ads
and bodysurfing the Internet, walking borrowed dogs
and joining humiliating support groups in the bleak
hope of bumping into someone who wouldn't be
caught dead there either. And Oscar had been one of

them. But no longer. He had waded through the litter of street fairs and the subtitles of foreign film festivals, forced himself to figure skate in winter and taught himself to rollerblade come spring, attended church and temple—and was done. He had decided. He would enlist in the ranks of the chronically lonely, and thus unlonely; embrace his solitude and thus cease to feel it. His father had lived all these years on his own, and there was dignity in that. Even a sort of contentment, he'd bet. It had to be better than the floundering struggle for more.

"Oscar? Sweetie?"

He lugged the manuscript down the hallway and into the copier room, ruffled and blew on both sides before dropping it in. Over the years he had become a connoisseur of such taskwork, a black belt in the martial art of getting stuff done. He hit Collate with his right thumb, tapped on Number of Copies with his left. He was a pianist in concert. A pilot in the cockpit. He adjusted the contrast lever under his pinky. After elbowing the Start button—a hockey goalie in the playoffs—he stepped back.

"Babycakes?"

"Be right there," he yelled over the chunking of the machine.

The office was only slightly calmer with the drowsy arrival of August. Most publishing executives were loafing at their beach houses and country retreats; but Dawn, who owned one of each, saw the daze of late summer as a chance to hotfoot it ahead of the competition. The season only seemed to raise her temper, and she leaned on her underlings with the violence of the sun.

"Oscar? I need to borrow your body."

"Coming."

He hauled himself down the hall to Marion's doorway, the warm stack of twelve copies cradled against his chest. Seated at her desk and sporting a plunging blouse, she was surrounded by half-written pitch letters, taped-up tour schedules, and snapshots of herself arm in arm with celebrity writers. Tacked to her bulletin board was a scrap of paper signed, during a slow moment at the Miami Book Fair, by John Grisham. Beside that was a cocktail napkin kissed, backstage at the David Letterman show, by Danielle Steele. The largest framed photo showed her squashed and grinning between Oprah Winfrey and the Tibetan monk who had become the first Dawn Books best-seller. The monk was looking sideways at the twin pontoons of Marion's breasts.

She ran a hand through her ruby-red hair and pointed at his papers. "Are those for Dawn? Is she out of that sales meeting?"

"Not yet."

"Thank God. How bad today?"

"Her mood? Hard to tell."

"Give it to me straight. On a scale of *civil* to — I don't know — *homicidal*."

"Grumpy," he judged.

"Grumpy's not good." A schedule flapped in her

hand. "I have to talk to her about this sixteen-city tour that's supposed to start next week. National TV. Major store signings. And the author won't fly."

"Isn't acceptable, you mean?"

"Refuses to travel by plane."

Despite her outrageous miniskirts and hourglass figure, Marion fell somewhere short of sexy. As the forty-year-old director of Dawn Books' publicity department, she was a soldier of the industry, a knight of the round conference table, and her clumsy feints at seduction did nothing to hide her greater passion for liaisons of the corporate variety. An unconvincing flirt and incorrigible gossip, clanking in her armor of peek-aboo half-shirts, she cantered from lunch to lunch in search of any rumor worth lancing and hoisting like a flag.

"Did you need me for something?" he reminded her.

"I do, Oscar. I need you. I want you." She was dialing her phone. She listened for a moment, changed her mind and hung up. Her fingers trailed provoca-tively, robotically, up her throat. "What's a handsome young man like yourself doing this weekend?"

"I have a wedding," he said. "In Maine."

"Another wedding?"

"Another college roommate."

"But I thought the last wed —"

"It was. And the one before that." He shrugged. "I had five college roommates."

"Sheesh. Someone should hire you as a reporter for the 'Aisle of White.'"

He blew upward at an itch on his nose. "What's that?" He was handsome, it was true, with boyish bangs and a gallant chin; only his height made too much of him, he had always felt with an embarrassment that matched the adolescent ache of his bones. Six feet tall at twelve years old, he had added an inch a year until graduation, another few centimeters in college. Simultaneously he'd developed a mitigating slouch—the cringe of a passenger on an up elevator out of control—that he corrected, now, to better bear the load of manuscripts.

"'Aisle of White?' It's that incredibly annoying magazine column about weddings. You've seen it. Every month a different couple with a new shtick: *Having met in the Caribbean, Fred and Wilma decided to have a pirate wedding!* The photo of Fred in the eye-patch. Wilma kissing the parrot. You've definitely seen it."

"I hate weddings," he said. "Why were you asking about this weekend?"

"Oh, nothing," she sang. She lifted her legs onto her desk and crossed fishnet stocking over stocking. "Nothing at all." She watched him roll his eyes. "I was just thinking of setting you up with someone."

"Not again."

"This girl's taller."

"Marion. Please. The last thing I want is to go out

with a fellow pituitary case and reminisce about our eleventh-grade basketball careers."

"She happens to be the cousin of a friend."

"I'm sure she's terrific," he said. "I'm just not doing that anymore. It's nothing against your cousin's friend."

"Friend's cousin."

"Whoever. I wish her the best. She should date someone who's dating. I'm not dating. I told you."

"I know you told me, Oscar. But it's not right." She fixed him with a stare. "Everybody dates."

"Not me."

"I see. And that's final."

"That's final."

The past year, in fact, had finalized it. The world can be divided into two types of people: those who get married and those who get more and more single; and it had become increasingly obvious that Oscar was one of the latter. The preceding few months had been a matrimonial onslaught, as every one of his former roommates paired off and settled down in a panic of flashbulbs while he looked on benevolently from a foot or so above. Four grueling extravaganzas in four states in as many months; tomorrow would make it five. He had never quite fit in with his roommates, and felt even less a part of the rented splendor of their occasions. The race to get married was a game of musical chairs, complete with hired music and assembled chairs, that he appeared to have lost without playing. He'd had girlfriends in high school and women friends in college, but the sudden silence of real life appeared to have scattered them in all directions but his. He was too polite to grab attention. Too tall to be seen. Too busy, these days, to bother and come up with a reason why not him. Tomorrow he would head to Maine to applaud the other type of people, the marrying type, for the very last time before returning to live out his single existence in a one-room apartment in the most pluralistic city on earth.

"I'm going to level with you." Marion took down her legs. "You're *nice*. You're *handsome*." She was tallying his traits on her painted fingernails. "You're *helpful*. You're *nice*."

"You already said nice."

"You're *tall*. Don't interrupt me."

He longed to set down the manuscripts; but that would have only prolonged his stay, with Dawn about to emerge from her meeting and assign him the ominous project she had mentioned more than once. It could be anything. Couldn't be good. A bandage that needed changing. A toilet that needed unclogging. His arms were exhausted. He held firm.

"My point is this: You're about the best guy around." She paused. "As a matter of fact, you're about the *only* guy around."

"Well, there's Carl."

"You see my point." She had lowered her voice. "You can't let yourself go to waste like that. You don't want to end up like Carl. You should be a hot prospect these days. You package yourself a little better, shop yourself around, and you'll generate interest. Believe me." She spoke of him as if he were a book proposal. "You'll get snapped up. Promise. Nibbles at first, few bites."

"Sounds painful."

"Could be, Oscar. It usually is. But how else are you planning to find someone?"

"Maybe I'm not planning to find someone."

"Everybody finds someone."

"Then I have nothing to worry about." His wrists were starting to cramp. "I really have to get moving, Marion."

"Yes, you do, baby," she said. "That's my point."

His desk was in the hallway, a shadowy cubicle by the bright threshold of the giant corner office that was Dawn's. This prompted employees like Marion and Carl to loiter frequently in his periphery, pretending at careless gab while they waited to bow and scrape before his boss. He pulled the manuscripts off his pile of them, binding each in turn with a stretched and twanged rubber band. As he worked, he couldn't help venturing a few more dreadful guesses at the project. She had lost her wallet, and he would be required to slay a cow, cure its hide, and stitch her a new one. She was plotting a romantic adventure with you-know-who—that was it, a trek up Everest—and he was to serve as her Sherpa. He was picturing himself waist-

deep in snow, head strapped to a trunk of white cloth-
ing, when Carl appeared from down the hall.

"Afternoon, my boy."

While Marion continued to strive to be chic, Carl
had long since tumbled into disrepair. He had lived in
his dingy office, griping and jotting at the pages
of books-in-progress, since the earliest days of the
company. He didn't appear to possess social acquain-
tances, to need the nourishment of outdoor air, to be a
citizen of the larger and less predictable world beyond
the building. This was his domain, these dung-colored
walls and fireproof carpeting. He carried himself with
a kind of stilted hauteur behind his foggy glasses,
despite his sour button-down shirts, beneath the pom-
padour of silvering hair that he lowered, now, in salu-
tation.

"She's not back yet," said Oscar.

"Not a problem." Carl held a copyedited manuscript, its pages slashed and curlicued with his gram-
matical corrections in red. He plucked a candy from
the basket at the corner of Oscar's desk. "Not playing
fetch today on Fifth Avenue, I see."

"Not today."

"Nevertheless, you found it. The ring." He popped
the candy into his mouth. "Good show."

"Thanks. How did you —"

"Marion told me everything."

Oscar stretched another rubber band around
another manuscript. "Marion tells everyone everything."

"Poor lad."

The phone rang sharply. "Hello, Dawn Books." He took the message from an L.A. agent begging to take Dawn to lunch. It rang again. "Hello, Dawn Books." He noted the apologies of her pedicurist, hoping to reschedule their appointment on Wednesday. "Hello, Dawn Books. Please hold. Dawn Books."

"Poor, poor lad."

These occasional gifts of pity were like punches to his stomach. It was a relief when Carl retreated to the far wall and changed the subject as he hung up the phone.

"Word has it that Dawn has purchased the rights to the autobiography of that—ahem. Rock singer."

"Yup. Tommy Gunn. Deal went through this morning."

"I presume that the agent," he said, "was Gordon Fox."

Oscar was careful to avoid any visible reaction to the name of you-know-who. He signed a cover card with Dawn's double-D and paperclipped it to the top manuscript, placed the package aside.

"And I suppose he charged a million."

"The advance? A million six."

"Yeegads. Agents are vultures, my boy. Never forget it. The scourge of the system. Eaters of their young. Hooligans with stationery. And Fox is the very worst of the lot. The man is responsible for more synergetic flops and multimediocre barbarities than the rest of them combined."

After signing and clipping the last of the notes, Oscar restacked the copies beside his phone. "You don't seem to share the excitement of the company on this one, Carl."

"As copy editor, I can only foresee a torrent of unnecessary commas and split infinitives. The author is an entertainer, need I remind you, and entertainers tend to express themselves rather, well, loosely. Unfortunately. In one-sentence paragraphs. With triple exclamation points." He tugged at the seat of his trousers. "*Night* without the *g* and the *h*. *You* without the *y* and the *o*."

"I get the picture."

"Although it could hardly be worse than this fiasco." He spanked the manuscript in his hands. "This will have to be sent back to the writer for another attempt at the English language. Dawn must be told. It's a travesty. A mockery." He lifted a page to examine the damage. "A botanist, this person. Atrocious."

Marion approached and slid a letter to be faxed into Oscar's In box. "Soon as you can," she instructed, pursing her lips in a kiss. She pointed past Carl at Dawn's doorway. "She back?"

"Not yet." The phone trilled again. "Dawn Books." He watched Marion line up against the wall beside Carl and wrinkle her nose discreetly. "Dawn's in a meeting right now. May I take— oh hey, Gordy."

He saw them both give a start. He lowered his head.

He had said the name out loud. Why had he said the name out loud? Quickly he unfolded Dawn's appointment book, walked his fingers through the weeks.

"The twenty-fifth, that's right. Until the twenty-eighth." The pages were a mosaic of commitments: black ink for business, blue for personal, tentative entries in pencil. "Super." He erased a sketchy gray weekend and made it blue. "I'll tell her. Thanks." He started to put down the phone and caught himself. "Me? Nothing. Going to a wedding." Small talk with the assistant, he thought: that bungling crowbar of a tool. "No, Maine. I know. Guy named Justin. Some kind of seaside theme. Yup. Lot of them lately. I seem to be at the age where— Right, right. So, good." He closed the book, worked through the patter. "Okay. She'll call you. What? No problem. You too. Sure thing." He fiddled with his tie. "You said it. All right, take care. Absolutely. You bet. 'Bye."

"*Gordy?*" Marion shouted as he replaced the receiver. She lunged forward to slap both hands on his desk. "As in Gordon? Gordon Fox?"

He concentrated on straightening the pens in his pen jar. How could he have said the name out loud?

"Answer me, Oscar. Level with me. I'm only asking because someone from Sterling Lord was asking *me* about it today at lunch."

"Asking you what?" Carl blundered into the discussion, his glasses askew. "Asking Oscar what?"

"About Dawn dating Gordon," she shot back.

"Gracious. Gordon the agent?"

"Gordon who just called. Who just spoke, at great length, to our good friend Oscar." She leaned closer. Her cleavage gaped. "Let's have it, kiddo. I work here too. I have every right to know absolutely everything about Dawn's sex life."

"I don't know what you're—"

"Bullshit." She was on to something, gripping it with her teeth in what might have otherwise looked like a smile. "I don't mean to pry," she said sweetly, "but if you don't tell me what the he— Hello!" She leapt away from his desk. "Oh, thank God. Dawn."

Dawn arrived as a bustle of white, striding between her employees and into her office.

"I've just got one—Dawn? Can I come in?"

"Ahem. Dawn?" Carl toddled into position beside Marion. "Might I inquire—Dawn?"

They stood in her doorway, grown-ups whimpering for attention, baby-stepping forward and back. Oscar took up her phone messages and calmly placed them atop her appointment book. He inserted a clean sheet of paper into his clipboard. Selected a pen. She crashed audibly into her chair. He stared at the unlit intercom button. A-one. And a-two.

Bwahhh.

"*Co*-ming," he called. He rounded his desk and headed for her door, walking past and above his coworkers and into the white-hot core of Dawn Books.

Marshmallow couch on mayonnaise carpet. Icy marble desk, bone-white table, bleached walls. Not a spot of color to muss that alabaster temple, apart from the rainbow spines of Dawn Books that filled the shelf against the back wall. Oscar spread her messages into a semicircle at the center of her desk.

"How was your sales meeting?"

"Fucking waste of time."

With her fashionably short hair and well-sculpted, resculpted face, Dawn gave the impression of faded and born-again beauty; of that strain of American royalty that runs, when injected, in the blood. Of the homecoming queen of some tedious hometown who left to win bigger stakes and fewer popularity contests in New York. She picked at the lapel of her cream-colored pantsuit. Tapped on the desk. She was looking for something.

"Where's my water? I had a water right here. Dammit, Oscar, what did you do with my water?"

"There's a new six-pack in your fridge."

She disappeared behind her desk. The door of her minirefrigerator opened and closed with a plastic smack. "Just make sure I have water, Oscar. That's the one thing I ask. A sip of water. I'm like a goddamned prisoner, begging for water." She cracked off the top of the bottle and drank desperately. "Where are my messages?"

"Right there."

"Where? *Where?*"

"Here." He reached forward and touched them. "And Gordy called."

"I know."

"He just want—"

"Shut up," she spat. "And shut the door."

Crossing the office and grasping the knob, he caught sight of Marion as she pretended not to be eavesdropping and set about adjusting a framed book cover on the wall. He pulled the door closed.

"You get that fish doctor on the phone?"

"Confirmed for Sunday morning," he said. "He'll be at your apartment at ten o'clock sharp. I have him booked on a flight from California Saturday night."

"And what's happening with *The Wonder of Wildflowers*?"

"Photos are in production. Text is in trouble."

"Trouble?"

"Carl said it's awful. No—atrocious."

"Who's Carl?"

"Carl," he laughed. "You know Carl. From down the hall. Carl the copy editor."

"Hell with him. Put it through."

"He said it needs another rewrite."

She glugged from the bottle. "So rewrite it."

"Me? Um, okay." He wrote that down.

"What about *Moonlight in Missoula*?"

"It's *Missouri*. And it's all set. I'll have the copies distributed by the end of the day."

Her cheekbones grew sharper. *"End of the day,* he says. Let me tell you something about the end of the day, Oscar. The day ends when I say it ends. And the day will *not* end until you carry out your goddamn *assignments*. That's the one thing I ask. I don't give a flying fuck about your weekend in Montreal."

"Maine."

"Jesus. Stop talking. Sit down, Oscar. *Sit*, for Chrissake." She watched him fold himself into the chair opposite her. "I can't bear to have you standing over me like a weeping goddamn willow. Shut up. Sit still. And pay attention. That's the one thing I ask."

As she looked over her phone messages, he looked over her. She was in good shape, he had to admit, the healthiest he'd seen her in ages. Dawn was that fearsome brand of Olympian woman who, after sprinting through the rat races and obstacle courses of male-dominated careerism, kicks over the hurdle of her fiftieth birthday and picks up speed. He had tracked her changes over the years from the close vantage point of a friend, albeit without the friendship, and this white stage suited her well. Her dark stage had been tiresome, marked by zombie eyeliner and funereal sweaters and by his trips to exchange her pitch-black boots for jet-black versions of the same model. Her floral fat stage, before that, had been an overblown response to the diet frenzy of the late '80s, when he'd started, his first weeks of work spent fetching her morning bran muffins and ordering crates of grapefruit. Aerobics had trotted in and out of the picture, along with his missions in search of leggings and Jogbras. Equestrianism had its moment, jodhpurs and all, as did therapy and botany; but the new Dawn had whited out all such dalliances. Gone were the kaleidoscopic distractions of her past, and in their place was a colorless focus on success.

And it was working. While soft-shoed whiners and harebrained pundits lamented the cerebral downfall of the book business, Dawn had set about profiting from it. She published and hustled books in every trend and genre: true crime, tell-all memoir, Jazz Age and New Age and antiaging inspirational. Her sales figures rose. Her personal income swelled. Her titles appeared on the *New York Times* best-seller list, her ghostly snapshot in *Publishers Weekly*. Before long she had grown her dainty book boutique into the most lucrative imprint of all the divisions of the various publishing houses of the famous multimedia conglomerate. Ever since Dawn had donned white, Dawn Books was in the black, and she saw no reason to change her ways.

"Fax these people and tell them no." She pushed a message slip across her desk. "No, no, no. Three faxes." She scrunched another slip into a ball and threw it at him. "And call these idiots back and tell them that we already did a big book on Asia—a cookbook, remember that piece of crap?—and it bombed."

"That's a no," he transcribed onto his clipboard, "to the biography of Mao."

"Now"—she clapped—"I need you to do something for me."

He smiled courageously. This was it. An officewide search for a missing filling from her tooth. A nationwide hunt for a clinical psychologist for her cat.

"I need you to get me a novel."

"A novel? Really? I can get you a novel." He

sprang to his feet. "No problem." On the contrary, he thought: this was unprecedented. An actual project after all this time. He could call several agents, assemble a line-up of writers. One of the few perks of his job was a Rolodex the size of a Ferris wheel. He would set up the deal. Get his name in the acknowledgments. A foothold on the ladder.

"It's up there," she said.

He traced a path from her finger to the top of her bookshelf.

"See it? Oscar. *Oscar.* You're not looking. Cardboard box."

"Oh."

"Thing's been here forever. Agent's called five times."

"He walked to the back of the office and reached upward past the shelves, careful not to nudge her white sculptures and knickknacks carved of quartz. The box perched above them was shoved almost to the wall. He grappled it off the edge and handed it over.

She blew a hole in its coat of dust and handed it back. "Add it to your pile this weekend. Rejection letter by Monday."

He knelt to gather the phone messages from around the legs of the chair and moved toward the door.

"Fuck are you going?"

"I'm going to get out those manusc —"

"Didn't I tell you I had something for you to do?"

"I thought it was —"

"Pull yourself together, Oscar. Concentrate. For one second. On me. If you can do that."

He gritted his teeth. Shifted his weight. Dreamed of an end to his endless job. But then came the softening of Dawn's chiseled face. Her eyes grew wide, beaming warmth—or at least a sort of haywire electricity—that rooted him helplessly to the spot. This is what happened, on cue, whenever he'd had enough. She melted like white chocolate, puddled and pleaded without having to say a word. Stirred into her expression was a generous understanding of all his faults, even an acknowledgment—perhaps there, in that glimmer—of one or two of her own. An apology for the ways of the world, for its necessary evils and regrettable imbalances. His shoulders sagged. He smiled back. The grip of her jaw had loosened, and she spoke.

"I'm getting married."

"What? You are?"

"Gordon and I are getting married." She seemed to be practicing the phrase.

"Oh my—"

"Shut up. This is top secret."

He could only nod.

"Time's right, both feel ready, yadda yadda yadda." She tapped a key on her keyboard. "So we're getting married."

It had all the romance of a corporate merger. Perhaps it was. Would they start their own agency, publish their own authors? Dawn Fox Books? "When?"

"Six months." She scowled at something on the screen. "Good round number."

"I meant when did he ask you."

"Just now. Eighth floor conference room."

"He's here?"

"Who."

"Gordy. Gordon."

"He's not here," she said. "I called him. After the sales meeting."

"The man proposed marriage on speakerphone?"

"Listen, Miss Manners. We're both busy people, as you may have noticed." She rapped on her desk. "Which is where you come in. I need you to plan this thing."

"What thing. The memo? The press release?"

"No press. Did you hear me say top secret?"

"Sorry. Yes, I did. Top secret."

There had been other top secrets. The time she'd left half a manuscript in the backseat of her limo, and he'd had to convince the author that it had been cut for the sake of narrative momentum. The time she'd been skewered in a writer's autobiography, and he'd had to take a razor blade to the offending page in the back corners of bookstores across Manhattan. The most recent top secret, his quick fib to Marion that Dawn's diamond ring had been inherited, was a relative cinch. He looked at it now, dazzled by its significance. The ring. Married. *Dawn.*

"Are you planning to invite people?"

"It's a wedding, Oscar. Are you listening? Can you hear anything from up there?"

"I just don't see how we can keep this top secret if—"

"Not *we*, Oscar. You. And yes, you *will* keep this top secret. If word gets out to Marion, it'll be all over the city."

"But it's a wedding. Word is supposed to get out."

"Not this wedding," she said. "Not now. Not when he has eight major clients with my publishing house and I have nine million bucks tied up in his agency and the last thing either of us needs is those prigs from the Authors Guild filing complaints about insider trading. Scavengers from the tabloids snooping around the office. Not when there's a deal to be made."

"You mean the Tommy Gunn deal? I thought that was signed this morning."

"Screw Tommy Gunn. I'm talking about something bigger. I'm talking about a deal that'll blow the— None of your business, Oscar. Don't ask me questions."

"Right."

"And don't ask my opinion. Don't try and drag me into this thing. This is *your* project, Oscar. Not mine. Yours. Start to finish. Soup to fucking nuts." Her face had hardened once more, eyes glinting metallically. "That is," she challenged, "if you want to keep your job."

He glanced about the room. He didn't. He did. He could quit right now by giving the answer he lived with, the answer he loved. But what then? He had no escape route, no backup plan. He had nothing—God help him—better to do. He had envisioned leaving too many times to count, had constructed and burnished his defiant farewell speech until the vowels shone. Yet it lay like an unused weapon, kicked aside again and again. He teetered in the middle of the office, wishing with all his gangly might for the strength not to say he did. Because he didn't.

He looked her in the iron eyes.

"I do."

The Date

"WEDDINGS A *GAH*-GEOUS," said the stout woman in the seat beside him. She peered over the peak of his knee. "Where ya from? Not from Maine."

"New Jersey. I live in New York."

"And off to a wedding, ya said."

"Right."

"*Gah*-geous."

The world can be divided into two types of people:

those who talk incessantly on airplanes and those who adamantly do not. Somehow Oscar always ended up sitting next to the former.

"And what a time of yeah for it. Don't get bettah weathah for a wedding." She looked out her portal window to admire the radiance of the heavens, the rug of clouds beneath.

"I can't stand August weddings."

He turned, startled. The third passenger in their trio of seats was a thin woman in a witchy black dress, pottery bracelets up both arms.

"You sweat off ten pounds by the time you get to the vows. Sunburn, sunstroke. Better keep an eye on the old folks," she warned. "Keep those water glasses full."

"Bettah now than February," replied the first woman. "Now *thah's* a challenge. Short month, crappy weathah. If ya thinking February, might as well wait till April."

Oscar pulled the napkin out from under his cup. He excavated a pen from his pocket.

"*Ah* got married in April. Twice," she went on. "Two April weddings. Two outta three. And every one of them"—she poked his arm: this was important— "in Maine."

He wrote "Maine" on the napkin to appease her. His hip had depressed the flight attendant call button with a reverberating bong, and he tapped it off.

"January and November," declared the other woman. "Snowed both times. I should have known right then I'd end up with two divorces." She threw up her hands with an exasperated clatter of bracelets. "Snow's a sign."

He had never understood what it was about being airborne that inspired such groundless conversations, turbulent confessions. Nor had he ever seen the sense in seating passengers according to class rather than height. He dug downward to find a sideways location for his foot, somewhere near the feet of the man in front of him. He would have liked to rest his elbows, but was too tightly sandwiched between the opinions of the women on each side of him, pinned by the urge of the previously married to toss their leftover advice and stale ideas like rice.

Select the clean snap of winter. Then again, there's the natural hoopla of spring. Sigh along with summer. Chuck the sturdier shoulder of fall. Keep in mind that the majority of couples marry from May through September, that Thanksgiving weekend can be hard to book too. Late winter is often soggy. October can freeze, drop of a hat. Dream of a sun-dappled lawn and lazy breezes; plan on festive umbrellas and backup sites. Know that weddings have been arranged and executed in a single day—and that four years would not be nearly enough, given the torrential brainstorms and flooding hysteria and last-ditch maneuvers of wedding season.

By the time he glimpsed, out the window, the upward approach of the earth, he had borrowed and covered all three of their napkins. He read them over as the plane bumped the tarmac and the brakes kicked in. "Welcome to Maine," grumbled the pilot over the loudspeaker. *To wedding hell,* said the napkins as he stuffed them in the pocket of his blazer and stood to thonk his head on the plastic ceiling.

The note-taking started immediately. It had to if she wanted to keep up with the event. She had to if she planned to have a column for December. *These are not your weddings,* her editor's voice droned in her head. *These are your job.*

She arrived an hour early to watch the setup. She penned a detailed sketch of a table, checked the spelling of the town. Having staked out the least conspicuous seat, she tilted back in her folding chair to size things up. Hundred and eighty, she guessed, and marked down a reminder to confirm. Her photographer wandered the grounds, triggering his light meter and squinting at the sun. The mother of the bride ventured over to offer her a drink. She declined, according to policy. Caught the woman by the back of the dress and changed her mind.

Then she flipped to a new page and bore down.

Fishing image in lead? Troll for mate / lure / snag / reel him in
Details: stones and sand dollars on tables, conch shell on bar,
loofah in portapotty
Justin and Wendy: met after college,
working for same firm, same floor
1st date: seafood? (ask best man—Kevin? Ken?)
Bridesmaids dressed as mermaids

Priest: Poseidon look-alike. On purpose?
(Neptune = Poseidon? check)
Mother of bride all in blue (humpback whale?) (no)
Mention "landscape worthy of Coleridge" / "Melville"
/ "Stephen King" (no)
Mention flower girl w/ seaweed bouquet
Don't mention smell

Oscar made his way across the lawn and under the
crowded tent, folding and unfolding a place card
shaped like a scallop. Place cards: There was something that hadn't occurred to him. Which would mean
a place card table. Place card table flowers. Place card
table flower vases. He should have brought his clipboard. The tables he passed were wrapped in lace,
grinning with silverware, laden with ingredients he
would have to preorder and assemble. High chairs and
ice tongs. Candles and candelabra. Beyond the loud
circles of people he saw a single vacant chair at the
table nearest the house, farthest from the view. The
Butt Table once again, he thought. He veered out from
under the tent to gather his goodwill one last time.

He stood alone on the stiff grass. Beaten gray by
the off-seasons, the shingled house of the bride's parents stood atop a hill that spilled downward in scrubby
greens and browns to the sea. The reception tent had
been erected on the flattest part of the lawn, around
the house from the smaller canopy that had sheltered
the ceremony. Apparently Wendy had grown up here;

but Oscar didn't know Wendy, knew next to nothing about Maine. He hardly knew Justin, for that matter, although as neighbors in their six-man suite for all four years of college they had argued toothpastes and test formats and pizza toppings almost daily. He turned his back to the guests who were milling and finding each other. Closed his eyes to the consoling wash of the sea.

"It's a lighthouse! It's the mast of a schooner! No, it's Oscar!" Somebody punched his hip. "Dude!"

He turned as a hand was lifted toward him. "Hello, Steve," he said. He went to shake it and had his palm slapped. "Rick." He slapped with the guy beside Steve.

"O-Man," Rick greeted him. As former captain of the lacrosse team, Rick tended to stand with his chest puffed and arm crooked before him—to scratch his stomach, or, as now, to hold a beer—as if he missed his stick. "How you been, dude."

"Not bad."

"Haven't seen you, what, since Stevie here tied the knot."

"Oregon." He nodded. "Three weeks."

"Dropping like flies," Steve said.

"Lambs to the slaughter," said Rick.

A third roommate, Gary, crossed the grass to join them. He carried a bottle of beer in one hand, a plastic cup of wine in the other. "It's the O-Man!" he yelled. Gary was something of a toy terrier, short-legged and eager to out-yip the rest of the pack.

"Gang's all here, bay-*bee!*"

"You still working at that bookkeeping job?" Steve asked.

"Book publishing. Yup."

"You know I've read every single book by Kirk Connolly?" boasted Rick. "I tell you that?"

"You did."

"Every one. Starting with *Mortal Reaction.* That was his first. Seen all the movies, too."

"What was the one with the Arab dudes?" asked Gary. "In the copters? They were like—*blam! I don't think so! Blam!*"

Rick answered over his beer: *"Lethal Invasion."*

"Or the one with the submarines? Where he was like, *You touch my wife? Wa-KAH! Wa-KAH!*"

"We don't actually publish Kirk Connolly," Oscar explained.

"You should," said Rick. "Stupid not to."

These reunions were hard for Oscar; not only because he felt so different from his former roomates, but because they made him feel behind. While Justin and Gary and Ricky and Stevie could all claim sniveling assistants to go with their six-digit salaries, he had to admit to being one—and for a fraction of the year-end bonuses lavished upon the moochers he used to help through their exams. They had stumbled into success, the way young men do: bumped into opportunities, mumbled through interviews, tromped a well-worn path to promotions and raises of their raises while Oscar continued to run circles for someone else. He didn't want their life, their coffee breath mingling with their aftershave, their monogrammed dress shirts and child-ish tales of bears and bulls. Still, it was increasingly dif-ficult to be proud of his.

"What's new with you guys?" he asked gamely. "Still traders?" There was so little to ask, only a few weeks after Oregon.

"Damn straight," said Gary. "Except for Ken. Where's Kenny? Kenny's on the buy side. Dumb jerk." He almost tasted the wine, switched hands to drink from his beer, and gagged as he spotted Justin's best man. "Ken-*nay!*" he cried. "There's the dude."

Seated beside the newlywed couple in the lemony glow of the tent, Ken could be seen making the moves on the costumed waitress—grabbing at her cardboard fins, making fishy kissing noises—who was trying to pour wine for the head table.

"Attaboy, Ken!"

"Bay-*bee!*"

"Where's his wife? Suzie. Susan." Oscar had only met her for a few seconds, months before at their wed-ding in North Carolina.

"Couldn't make it," said Rick. "Lucky bastard. That's all you, Ken Doll!"

Oscar searched for the rest of the wives and found them wilting at a table nearby. He waved a hand. Nobody waved back. Gary held out the cup of wine as a promise to one of them—Emma, Emily—and let it fall to his side, undelivered, before turning back to the men.

"Justin," he said. "Last one to fall." He made a kind of salute with his beer. "You believe this, dude? We're all *married.*"

The three of them hit each other's bottles. Oscar, having nothing, gave a smile.

"How sweet is that?" Steve said.

"Sucks," answered Rick.

They talked that way for a few minutes, sidling back under the tent as caterers jogged around them with salads. Oscar nodded at their news. Work sucked, but the money was sweet. A receptionist at Rick's office was sweet. Buying an apartment sucked. The Yankees sucked this season, the Knicks would be sweet next year. He nodded and nodded. These guys hadn't changed; and yet they appeared to be softly falling apart, the way things do when left in water. Heads of hair were eroding, chins doubling, stomachs starting to spread. Already their fourth fingers bulged around their wedding rings, choked by the bind. They had all gotten married with the same groggy mob mentality with which they used to shuffle down to breakfast at the dorm: hurrying and punching each other to get there, sullen once they did. He watched them head off to their table and scoot in reluctantly beside their wives.

The ocean stretched forever, a patient green. The bartender was wearing a snorkel and mask. Oscar ordered a beer and wove through the chatter and cup-clinks toward his place at the Butt Table.

• • •

While much is made of the Head Table in the dutiful arrangement of a standard wedding, the Butt Table is rarely mentioned. Yet it's always there, and just as carefully planned: a circle of outcasts quarantined off behind the stage, beyond the shrubbery, in the half-light of the back room. A freakish colony of them, the unenthusiastically invited. Here sat the wedding professionals, having fought through the barrages of personal checks intended to drive them away. The florist, for instance, digging up praise for her droopings of ivy and azalea. The harrumphing minister himself, all out of speeches and hogging the bread. Look no further for the twisted branches of extended family that would be better lopped off: the great-aunt kept alive by her racist tirades; the glum half-stepbrother who found himself in cockfighting. This was Oscar's barren hometown in the geography of the American wedding, falling as he did, or else swept for the sake of neatness, between the cracks. Five for five, he thought. He pulled in his chair until his shin hit the center post. Never again.

To his left an ancient man had fallen asleep. To his right a young woman appeared to be preparing her toast. Lightly tanned arms bracketed her scribblings in a notebook, a strap of blue sundress wandering off her shoulder. Turning away from her with some difficulty, he noticed that the table—strewn with an assortment of shells and mounds of beach sand—was a dump.

"Bride or groom?" called out a red-faced man with flip-up sunglasses from across the table.

"Me? Neither." He pushed away the starfish that abutted his salad plate. "I'm a friend of—I know Justin."

"Groom, then!" He raised his glass. "I'm bride."

Oscar lifted his beer. Everyone else was twisted away in their chairs, gazing toward the tinkle of better tables. All but the woman in the sundress, who stopped writing, just then, to face him.

"So how do you know Justin?" she asked.

"I, um."

She was astonishingly pretty, with enormous brown eyes and sun-streaked hair piled carelessly on top of her head. Her page was a mess of notes, fingers drumming, pen aloft—but he didn't see any of them, having lost all peripheral vision to the staggering appeal of her face. It occurred to him that he had forgotten the question.

"Did I—sorry?"

"How. Do. You. Know."

"Justin," he finished for her. "Wait, how *do* I—oh, I'll tell you. I know Justin because we went to school together."

"Aha."

"College," he said. "Roommates."

There was a buzzing in his chest. A numbness about the legs.

"Roommates. One *m*."

"Two."

"Just you and Justin?"

"No, there were six of us." He noticed the movement of her pen. "Are you taking notes?"

"Six. That's great. So, let's see." She clicked her pen twice. Twice again. "Would you say he was . . . neat?"

"Who, Justin?" Her eyes grabbed for him, and he looked for somewhere else to look. "That would be no," he informed the pale face of a cucumber.

"Really? Downright revolting? Or just, say, casual."

"I'll say casual."

"Be honest."

She must have leaned closer, as he could smell something quite different, something lovelier, than brine. "Let's put it this way." He worked to spear a cherry tomato with his fork. "For three years we all thought he had a dog. Until one of us finally called it."

She laughed. It was a perfect laugh: the shattering of fake china, the fall and smash of a leased chandelier. He dared to look up. Her cheeks were flushed, eyes brimming. "And it didn't come," she managed.

"No, it did," he said. "That was the scary part."

She fell forward again with a glorious snort. The whole table had turned to watch them, even the old man revolving in his chair, although Oscar was unaware of their presence. He placed the tomato in his mouth with a hidden burst that matched his own.

The first dance took place on schedule, Justin guiding his bride around the dance floor and pumping a fist at his friends. The deejay had a handlebar mustache, fish-shaped tie, and a habit of throwing his microphone hand-to-hand and interrupting the Cindy Lauper song

with: "And *Wendy* just wants to have fu-un! Yow!"
Eventually he handed the mike over to Ken, who stammered through a series of best-man clichés (Justin as one of the guys, Wendy as part of the gang) before sitting to receive the merciful pats of his wife. Lobsters were served and wrestled to pieces. And in a distant corner of the proceedings, the Butt Table got drunk.

In the companionable spirit of refugees marooned together, they learned each other's names and occupations amidst an emergency distribution of drinks. Wendy's father's lawyer obtained an armful of iced beer from the nearby rowboat filled with them. Justin's family dentist swiped two bottles of wine from the teetotaling table behind her, two more when a waiter replaced them. Lauren had seen it happen before, although she usually was careful to take no part. This time she swigged from a bottle of white wine and tilted toward Oscar.

"Know how they met?" She leaned an elbow on a mussel shell and cracked it.

"I don't."

"At the office," she said. "Worked in the same office. How's that for luck."

He grabbed himself a fourth beer, or possibly a fifth, from the dripping assembly at the middle of the table. He opened it with his lobster cracker. Took a long swallow for strength.

"Ran into each other at the water cooler," she went on. "Second day there. He gets up to get a drink. She happens to get up at the same time. And wham."

"Sounds easy," he said. Thinking: *Wham.*

"Easy? I'd call it impossible. I mean, if you have to be in the same corner of the same floor of the same building at the exact same time to meet someone, then fat chance."

He jutted his elbow onto the table a short distance from hers. "Maybe they would have met anyway."

"I think not." She set the bottle aside and pulled out her notes. "Wendy likes to play tennis and go sailing and see old movies. Justin likes to play video games and go to strip clubs and watch football. She loves shopping for new clothes; he wears the same hockey jersey every weekend. She was looking for a man who would dote on her forever. He made a pass at me a few seconds after we met." She closed the notebook. "According to empirical evidence, Oscar, this couple's qualities and interests intersect at that water cooler."

"And you're thinking of putting that in your toast?"

"Hell, I'm thinking of renting a water cooler." She drank again from her bottle. Knitted her brow. "What toast?"

"You're making a toast!" gasped Maggi, craning toward them from across the table. Lauren had asked her to spell her name (no *e*) and to state her occupation: she was the makeup artiste (extra *e*) responsible for Wendy's lipstick and mascara. "I love the toasts. Toasts are like the best part."

"Toasts," said Lauren, "are the very worst part."

"Who *are* you? What are you going to *say?* I'm like the expert on toasts."

"I'm not saying anything."

Maggi had squirmed almost out of her seat. "You're not? Why not? You totally should!"

"Not allowed to. I'm invisible at these things."

"I know the feeling," Oscar heard himself say.

Lauren was staring out at the ocean. "You can't imagine," she replied.

Wendy and Justin had set out on tour, side by side, table by table. Their faces showed the strain as they shook hands, kissed cheeks, and moved each other along. Across the tent Steve knocked over a glass to a ripple of applause. The deejay played "Rock Lobster" for the second time. "But it wasn't a *rooock,*" he sang into the mike. "It was Justin's . . . *fatherrr!*" — and he pointed to a boutonniered man at the bar who irritably waved him off. The train of Wendy's dress caught under someone's chair leg. Once it was freed, she laughed gaily.

"I hate weddings," Oscar said.

"You can't hate weddings," Maggi objected. "Nobody hates weddings. That's like hating *birthdays.* Or *funer—*"

"*You* can't hate weddings," Lauren agreed with a wave of her wine bottle. "Only I can hate weddings."

Down! Down! the deejay was shouting.

"Sorry?" Oscar asked her.

"You can't hate weddings until you've been to seventy-five of them. Not until you're breathing but-

tercream and eating honeymoons, until you're strangled by tulle and smothered by—"

"See that table over there?" he cut her off. "Right
there. Navy suits." He nodded confidently. "Been to
every one of their weddings. Thank you very much.
All this year."

She counted. "That's three."

"Plus the best man's. And this one. That makes
five."

She banged down her bottle like a gavel. "I said
seventy-five, Oscar."

"You can't be serious."

"Seventy-six in a couple weeks. Las Vegas."

"Come on."

"Seventy-seven the month after that. Hot-air balloon."

It was then that he realized she was the only member
of the table who hadn't mentioned her job; and that he
was the only one who knew it. "You're a writer," he said.

After all these years in their company, he was
quick to recognize writers. There was a gaping open-
ness to them, unsuccessfully hidden by bluster. They
would saunter into the office, cloaked in their look—
scarves for the romance queens, fedoras for the
reporters—and stark naked in spite of the getup. They
were missing material, lacking edges and angles.
Striving to cover their subjects, they couldn't help bar-
ing themselves. Lauren was one of them, no doubt
about it, her entire life in her eyes. The dress strap
slipping again down her arm. But different.

"I'm a wedding columnist," she said. She told him the name of the magazine.

"Really? What kind of weddings?"

"Theme weddings. Dream weddings. Extrao-*or*rdinary weddings," she said, spilling extra syllables.

A woman at the next table spoke up. "You're Lauren LaRose."

"Ohmygod." Maggi was hopping in her seat. "Ohmygod. You're the 'Aisle of White' lady. I'm like the most humongous fan of 'Aisle of White.' You're Lauren LaRose? No you're not. Is this going to be in 'Aisle of White'?"

"Boat weddings, farm weddings. Country western, medieval, Casablanca." She was talking to Oscar. "Month after month." She took another slug of wine. "I'm having a career crisis."

"Don't worry," he said. "They pass."

"How long have you been at your job?"

"Ten."

"*Years?*" She lifted toward him.

"Ten years last week."

"Wowee. Did they give you anything?"

"For ten years? Nothing."

"You're supposed to get tin on your tenth anniversary. That's the rule," Lauren said. "I know all the rules. Tin on your tenth. Ten on your tinth."

"So what do you get for seventy-five months?"

She smiled. "Exhausted."

"Well, cheers." He held up his beer and tapped it against her bottle.

"Cheers, Oscar. To our awful anniversaries."

His hand was braced on the table and she brushed it with her fingers before downing more wine. He upended his beer and almost toppled backward with it.

Nightfall, then, with the crabby smell of the ocean and the deterioration of the party above it. Ordinarily Lauren would have left before that, the sand castle cake having been cut and the crowd thinning, her photographer long since escaped to their budget hotel. Bride and groom had been dispatched beneath a volley of tossed shells. The best man and his pals had climbed into the boat of beer and were pretending to paddle. But tonight she did not disappear. The table had emptied save Maggi, who, when she shrilled a battle cry and made for the dance floor, left Oscar and Lauren alone to watch the last dying logs of color over the ocean.

"Can I ask you a question?"

"Sure thing," she said.

"Let's say you're planning a wedding."

"Let's not."

"Okay."

He played hockey for a minute with the side of his hand and a clam shell. He could eat more cake—he could pretty much eat forever—but wasn't about to get up in front of her and lumber monstrously for the dessert table. While seated he appeared standard size. If he stayed put, he might stand a chance. He slumped until he was her height.

"I'm sorry," she said. "I have a thing about weddings. Forget I said that. So you're planning a wedding. What's your question?"

"You sure?"

"Fire away."

"I just wanted to ask how one might, um"—he gesticulated vaguely—"start."

"I wouldn't," she advised him. "Once you start you can't stop."

"Let's say I have to."

She blew out through her lips with a sound like a motorboat. "Indoor or outdoor?"

"Got it. So you start with location."

"That was a question, Oscar. When is it?"

"When's what?"

"Your wedding."

"I don't have a wedding. But, right, say I did. Do. In March."

"Then it's indoor."

"Is it?"

"You'd prefer outdoor."

"Me? I don't care. I'm just wondering."

"Ha. Sure. Just wondering." So he was engaged, she thought. Of course he was. Why wouldn't he be? "To answer your question, you set the date. That's your first step."

"A date," he said. "That much I have."

"Then the place."

"Okay. That's next."

"Just take it step-by-step. Once you have the

place, get your minister. When you have the minister, arrange for the food. Then you can tackle the flowers and the band and all the rest. One task at a time. Think of them as chapters. You're in publishing. They're just complicated, endless chapters."

"Thanks."

"Step-by-step," she repeated. She pushed away her plate. The breeze had picked up and been stripped of its warmth. From far offshore came the planking of a buoy. First interesting guy she meets at a wedding—despite the enduring, infuriating myth about weddings—and he's engaged. Behind her she could hear the next table talking about this month's column. They were getting it all wrong. The couple was Scottish, not Irish, and had passed out kilts, not skirts, at the reception. She sat forward. "I'm having a career crisis."

"You mentioned that." He felt like touching her arm. A fidget to his right and he'd be touching it.

"I can't do this anymore. I have nothing more to say about the depth of other people's feelings or the number of layers on their stupid cake." She flopped open her notebook. "Look at this. These are all the notes I have."

He moved toward her in hunched jumps, the grass making it difficult, as he gripped the chair beneath him and stabbed the legs closer, to avoid standing up and scaring her off.

"This look like a column to you, Oscar?" She pointed at the wild haiku of parenthetical guesses and question marks. "Forgot to interview the family. Never talked to the caterers. Can't even remember the couple's song. I have a grand total of about two paragraphs here."

"'Octopus's Garden.'"

"Was it? The song?" She scratched it in at the bottom of the page. "I'm a wreck."

Now would be an excellent time to touch her arm, he thought. But it was miles away, unbreachable inches away.

"Not supposed to reveal my identity. Not supposed to drink. *No chatting. No dancing.*" She spoke in a husky voice, mimicking someone.

"No dancing?"

"I'm the reporter here, Oscar. Fly on the wall. Eye on the ball. *These are not your weddings, Miss LaRose. These are your job,*" she said gruffly. "Well, I'm tired of my job. I'm tired of these not being my wedding. Ha. Whoops."

But he hadn't heard, too busy reading her notes. "It's all here, Lauren. You have the ingredients. I like the Stephen King idea. You just have to organize it better. Tell you what." He took up her pen, looked at her squarely. "I'll help you with your writing if you help me with my wedding."

"You don't want to make that deal."

"Sure I do."

He did, in fact, although he hadn't thought to say it before the sentence hung twinkling between them like a string of lights.

"Trust me on this, Oscar. You'd be getting the short end. I'm a columnist. That's every month. Article after article. They're unending."

"That's what you said about a wedding."

"But I could give wedding advice in my sleep. Weddings are what I do."

"And editing is what I do. Here." He glanced over the page, drew a few lines and arrows. "See, that right there is your setting." He circled it. "And this is all about the decor. And there's the love story part. Separate that out. I'd start with the love story. Which will lead right into setting." The paragraphs shaped themselves before him, solid and well-rounded like stones in a wall. "All these minor details belong together: Porta Potties, tables, song. Just add a sentence to introduce them. Then put your quotes at the end."

"I don't have any quotes."

"I'll give you a quote. You just need someone to say something that brings it back to love. And you're finished."

"I'm finished all right." Doubtfully she read it over. "Hey." She sat up straight. "This works. And you'll give me a quote? On love? This is actually going to work."

"Step-by-step." He smiled and held out her pen.

She clasped his whole hand around it. "You've got yourself a deal."

The deejay was calling people onto the floor for a last group dance. He demonstrated the moves: a spin, three claps, a side step and shoulder-jiggle. Lauren watched Maggi strive to keep up with the teenagers, clapping off-beat. A grandmother turned the wrong way and was yanked back into line. Seventy-five weddings, she thought, without a dance. She had even ceased tapping her foot. She was weaving in her chair, however; nothing to do about that. Seventy-five weddings without a drink, and now this.

"Can I ask you another question?"

"Sure can," she said. "That's the deal."

"What would you rather be doing?"

"Than this?"

"Than the column."

She shrugged. "I'd like to write a book."

"Good for you. You should."

She laughed. "Yeah, me and every other New Yorker who's ever smoked a menthol cigarette and sat in a SoHo café with a brand-new journal and the age-old conviction that—"

"I'm serious," he said. "You should. The column gives you a head start. That's a built-in following. A national magazine means coast-to-coast exposure. I can see it at sales conference. The reps would go ballistic."

"Come again?"

"The reps. Sales reps. That's where books are launched, at sales conference. The publisher introduces the book to salespeople from all over the country, who then fan out to put it in stores nationwide. It would be a breeze to launch a name that's already in print every month. Especially a name like Lauren LaRose."

"Oscar's a nice name. I like it. *Oscar.* What's your last name?"

"LaRagweed," he said. "Not as good."

"Shut up."

"It's LaGrouch."

She collapsed forward onto the table, her head touching down and shaking. When she came back up, her forehead was plastered with sand.

"It's Campbell. You have—"

"What." She touched her cheek. "What." Flicked at her hair.

"Nothing. Here." He reached toward her—was he doing this?—and gingerly dusted above her eyebrows. She closed her eyes. "Sand?"

"Just a little." It rained onto her plate. Her eyelids were eggshells, lips shut tight like a little girl's. He could not remove his hand from her face. Back and forth, back and forth, even more gently now. At last he pulled away. "There you go."

But her eyes were still closed. The dance ended in a flurry of handclaps and kneebends. Her shoulder nudged his and she didn't pull it away. She was breathing deeply. He inflated with her breath, deflated without it. He thought of hoisting an arm around her shoulders; but the limb, as he attempted to lift it, was as unwieldy as a lobster claw.

The deejay turned off his mike with an electric bloop. Staff members in red antennae had begun to collect plates. Gary shouted something in Oscar's direction, leaning out from the departing crowd. Rick made an intricate and obscene motion with his fist and palm. The next sound was Oscar's, although it seemed to drift in from elsewhere like the noise of the sea.

"Do you want to dance?"

Lauren opened her eyes. "I can't."

"Okay."

"It's not that I don't want to," she said. "I just can't."

"No problem."

"It's a rule. My editor's pretty strict about that. I'll lose my objectomy. My objiclivity." She giggled, shuddering their shoulders.

Past the overturned tables and unstrung lights, some guy was pulling up the puzzle-piece squares of dance floor and loading them into the flatbed of a pickup truck. Six pieces of floor remained. Then five. Across the near-empty tent, a man in a tuxedo signaled to them that it was time to go.

Four.

Three.

"I really want to, Oscar," she said. "I just can't."

Two.

"Not unless you're big enough to beat up my editor."

At which point he stood—back straight, head held high—to her gasping laughter. And he dragged her, and she dragged him, toward the last square foot of romance above the dark scramble and boom of the sea.

The Place

"*H*ELLO?"

      "Oscar. Me."

He cleared his throat. Rubbed his face. "Me who?" Although he knew.

"*Me* me. Do re goddamned me."

He looked at the woozy digits on his bedside clock. "It's seven in the morning, Dawn." He thought for a second. "And it's Saturday."

"Good for you. Next question. Name the book that hits stores today."

"Today? *Killer Mountain*."

"Wrong, hotshot. *Angry Ocean*."

"Actually, it's *Killer Mountain*. *Angry Ocean* goes on sale next month, along with *Terror of the Tundra*. We're shrink-wrapping them together as a disaster book promo. Remember that memo from special sales?"

"Gotcha," she said. "You're awake."

"I'm awake," he admitted. Across his apartment, through the slim single window, the sky was turning a more hopeful shade of gray. No one was awake.

"And where are you going?"

"Back to sleep."

"Like hell you are, Oscar. You're going to the stores."

"No bookstore is open at this hour."

"Will be soon enough. And what are you going to do there?"

He heaved himself into sitting position. "Turn the book cover-out on the shelves. Plant a half dozen by the cash registers. Couple in the bathroom. Sneak one into the Recommended section. Dawn, I do this every pub day. I'm perfectly aware—"

"You are perfect," she said, "at nothing."

He exhaled into the phone. He heard her breathe back. They were a married couple, God help him, croaking at each other first thing in the morning; only from different beds in different neighborhoods, leading dissimilar lives on opposite edges of the city. Poor thing, he thought, imagining her and her insomniac morning in her underdecorated penthouse on the Upper East Side. And then, like a henpecked husband: Poor me.

"I have to go to the store anyway," he said. He was standing now, pulling the covers off his futon. "I have to find a book on weddings that might give me some idea about a place."

"Not *the* store, Oscar. *Every* store, Oscar. Chains, independents, the tables on the damn sidewalks."

"I know."

It sounded as if she was getting up too. "If you know so much, Oscar, then why do you need me to call and remind you? You don't think I've got better things to do? It's seven-o'-fucking-clock in the morning."

"Is it?" he asked. "I had no idea. Terribly sorry to bother you. I was just heading out to the bookstores."

"Yes you were," she said. "Yes, you goddamn were."

Beyond Inspiration, to the right of Etiquette, is a section of the bookstore thickly frosted in whites and blues. Yet their soft-focus covers cannot lessen the weight of those tomes, nor lighten the prissy fierceness of their commands. *Plan the Perfect Wedding! Execute the Wedding of Your Dreams!* Shelves and shelves of expertise, dust-jacketed tons of instruction; but after a morning spent paging through every option in the store (*Tie the Knot! Jump the Broom!*), Oscar could see

he'd come up empty. There were directions for
Christians, traditions for Jews, guidelines for the Irish
and African; but not a word of advice for the calm or
the lackadaisical, no pointers for those looking to
fudge their way through. Several books were spiral-
bound, promising convenient handfuls of nuts and
bolts—and unleashing more severe checklists, rigid
laws, and reproach. Volume after volume delineated
the fanatical crafting of a flawless occasion, but there
was nothing to help him throw one together with ease.

His eyesight was bleary as he left the wedding
shelves and walked across the store. He threaded a
route through New Fiction, around Best-Sellers, and
in and out of Self-Improvement before locating the
escalators past the neon café. On weekends, even at
this hour, these megastores were a riot. Women set
upon the relationship paperbacks, scouring *The
Hustling Husband* while keeping an eye on the leggy
blonde reading *Cheating for Keeps*. Men browsed the
swimsuit calendars and dawdled haughtily in
Literature before convening in the checkout line with
the same basic blockbuster under all their arms. A
hundred thousand new titles a year in America, two
hundred thousand in the building, and shoppers
responded like lab rats to the one or two preselected
by CEOs. People were willing to read the novels of
James Baldwin once they were fit on place mats for
Black History Month and sold along with the Ralph
Ellison mugs and Toni Morrison's favorite tea. Never
before had such throngs read poetry, albeit as poetical

fridge magnets. No one could resist a book that had been a movie before being animated for television and immortalized as toys. This was the book business at the turn of the twenty-first century: a vast experiment of pushed buttons and carefully timed tie-ins. And if it left Oscar longing for art, he could find it between Accounting and Audio. Should he pine for more romance, there were tabletop pyramids of it by the drinking fountains on three.

He hunkered in a corner and opened the binder he'd swiped from the tenth-floor supply room and covered with a false Foreign Rights label. He pinched and flipped open the tab marked Location to read what Lauren had told him about finding a place.

The goal, like that of architects, is to conjure a space out of spirit; to match two souls with four walls that will house your greatest vows. Home would be easy—and always edgy. Churches are churches, no choice. But a barn has the earthy appeal of a hoedown, an atmospheric reminder of the squawking manual labor of love. A ship suggests a journey, a horse-drawn carriage a jerkier ride. A restaurant would do nicely, if it didn't overemphasize the food. Botanical gardens are blissful, apart from sneezing fits and bees. There were pages of her suggestions, her voice drifting upward from the thicket of his handwriting like the wind through trees. *Mansions*, she had whispered as she clutched his back for balance. *Libraries*, she'd breathed when he dipped her low over the salty grass. He had spun her away, pulled her deftly back as the tables were folded and rolled past their tiny platform, the Porta Potties towed toward their truck. He closed his eyes to hear the music of that clearance, the unmistakable rumble of change.

Her apartment was a disgrace. Not repulsive or offensive, but a literal disgrace, with its shameful lack of light and humiliating dimensions, the approximate size and ambiance of a maximum security jail. Her plants sat beneath a dim window on death row. The heat clanked like a chain gang. And the end of the summer—it was September already—brought the slow water torture of a leaky AC. Her hatred of housecleaning didn't help, the floor riddled with rice cake wrappers and the corpses of sweatshirts; nor did her job, overfilling her only closet with columns of past columns. Still, it was the only apartment she'd lived in since moving from Idaho nearly eight years before, and as a rent-controlled one-bedroom, it was cheap enough to inspire allegiance. This was how people lived in New York City, she'd learned. They unfold themselves every morning from Houdiniesque hovels, take a last deep breath of the night air before wedging themselves back inside.

She left the premises with the sense, by now familiar, that she'd cobbled together her very last article. She was out of ideas, empty of words. By the time she hit the echoing iron stairs, she was considering law school. No, business school. Wait: no school. An opening sentence occurred to her as she clapped down to the lobby.

Joanna "JoJo" Hunter, 29, may have gazed with apparent longing at every one of her patrons while she danced, kicked, and gyrated onstage as an adult entertainer in the heart of Las Vegas; but she only had eyes, under those false eyelashes, for one guy.

Then came an image to follow it—the slow striptease of love—and a joke about the garter toss for the end. She had practically finished the column by the time she stepped out into the sour beer smell of noon in the East Village. She went through this every time, the failure and triumph and ultimate letdown of writing for a living. It was Saturday. Her deadline wasn't until Tuesday. But next weekend was the aeronautical wedding in Kansas for which she ought to have started her phone interviews already. Monday she would focus, she swore to herself. Tomorrow she'd recuperate. And today, if all went according to plan, she'd meet men.

She turned left off her stoop, avoided a cartwheeling newspaper, and headed down the block. Three dates in a day was a terrible idea. It had seemed genius back when she'd accepted and aligned them, spurred to action by a slow dance with a tall guy in Maine. Determined, from that evening onward, to find one of her own. In a single day, a single outfit, she would efficiently explore a wide range of options, reject them all with a triple sigh of dismay. These nonwedding weekends of hers were precious, after all, and this had seemed a good way to make the most of one. Although at the moment it seemed like a nightmare. Lunch with Bill—no, lunch with Marco. Then down to Bill in SoHo. Up to Chris in Chelsea. She was tired already. She picked up the pace.

If seventy-six columns of women could find someone, so could she.

A pianist in pearls was tickling the ivories as Oscar entered the hotel. Two gentlemen in cravats were reading the *Wall Street Journal* at two of a dozen marble tea tables. As he walked past them, the piano notes paddled upward and high overhead like birds in a cathedral. *A cathedral*, he thought; and just as quickly decided against it. Dawn wouldn't take kindly to any architectural grandeur that rivaled her soaring sense of self. A hotel made more sense, featuring on-site employees at her beck and call, a chef at her disposal. Plenty of private rooms where her assistant might hide. He continued through an archway and up a carpeted set of stairs, where the caped and hatted reception staff directed him to the banquet office.

"The first question, sir," said the liaison who met him there, "is one of numbers." He was in his early thirties, with a trimmed goatee and a double-breasted suit and the seeing-eye-dog technique, as they walked through the hotel, of bumping Oscar on the arm when he wanted him to turn corners. "How many guests do you two envision?"

"Well, it's not us two. It's not my wedding. I think I mentioned that on the phone. I'm setting this up for my boss."

"Of course. And your boss is—"

"—busy," he said.

"Yes. But who is he."

"He's a she. Beyond that, I'd rather not say."

"She's famous, in other words."

"Not today she's not."

"As you wish. Certainly, sir. All right, then." With this spritz of mystery into the stale air between them, the man was invigorated. Walking more briskly, he body-checked Oscar into the threshhold of a tremendous ballroom. Round chandeliers floated like jellyfish beneath the ripples of an ornate ceiling. The tables were set for some imminent occasion, spangling with knives and forks and fanned by napkins. "As the premier luxury hotel in Manhattan, we handle *many* celebrity weddings." He flared his fingers about the room. "The Emperor Room."

"Very nice."

"Marble wainscot and pilasters, nickel silver railings, the works. Is she in television?"

"My boss? I can't tell you. What are pilasters?"

"There was a television wedding here just last weekend, as a matter of fact. Do you watch *One Life to Live*?"

"Nuh-uh."

He fingered his facial hair. "Let's head over to the Jade Room."

Oscar was butted down the hall and up a carpeted staircase and through a doorway to the Jade Room. Even larger than the Emperor Room, its walls were padded with green fabric and overhung with cream-colored balconies that looked as if they were carved out of cake.

"Only two-tiered ballroom in New York," bragged his guide. "And the only four-story ballroom in the world." He leaned sideways. "She's a singer."

"I'm not telling. Are those things pilasters?"

"If I am to help you stage your event, sir, I simply *must* know the person I'm staging it *for*. Rest assured, the hotel caters to famous patrons all the time. Did you happen to see *Batman Two*?"

He shook his head.

"Nonetheless, sir, I *will* need a number."

"My number?"

"Number of guests."

"Right. Guests. Good question. I'm actually not sure."

"You're not."

"Well, it isn't my wedding," he said. "As I told you."

"But she must have given you some idea. A general conception. An approximate *feel*," the man fumed.

"She did, she did." Oscar thought it over for a minute. "I'd say around ten."

"Ten . . . people."

"It should be small. Ten is small, isn't it?"

"Ten is small." He folded his pin-striped arms.

"Ten is *too* small. I can't show you anything for ten."

"No?"

"Ten is not going to fill a ballroom, sir. The average person, in a banquet-style setup, ought to be allotted twelve square feet. You're talking about a need for only one hundred and twenty square feet. This room measures four *thousand.*"

"Who did those calculations?"

He lifted proudly onto the toes of his loafers, his head at Oscar's chest. "Those are the figures, sir. In a theater-style setup, each guest needs only nine square feet. That's row after row, side-by-side, no eating or activities. Conference-style, you're looking at twenty-three feet a person. Room to take notes, look over handouts, what have you."

Oscar's brain was reeling. He wasn't used to being so ill-informed. He was a master of this sort of minutiae, with a head for facts and a knack for procedure; but in this case a total blank. He knew nothing about weddings. He *hated* weddings—that's right—or at least he had until Maine. There ought to be mass-mailed instructions, he thought, as there were for jury duty and income tax. There had to be a way to track down Lauren. He could look in the magazine. They would have a number to call. He could just call the number. He looked at the man. A number.

"How about a hundred and twenty people?" he offered. "That would be, what, fourteen hundred—"

"Not in the Jade Room. Not even close. Cotillion Room, maybe."

"*Two* hundred and twenty. That's what she told me. I remember now."

"Two-twenty is not a *small* wedding. I believe you said *small,* sir."

"That is small," he replied with a meaningful look. "For her."

"She's in movies."

"Getting warmer."

"Sports."

"Cold."

He tugged at his tuft of beard. "Let's have a look at the Pegasus Room."

It was not as large as the others but just as outlandishly garnished. Although the round wooden tables were bare at the moment, the room was otherwise plush with carpeting and resplendent with brass banisters, antique wall fixtures, and something that looked like a gigantic spittoon.

"This, as you can see, would be a bit more manageable for two hundred. You're looking at five foot rounds—"

"Those are tables, I take it."

"—seating eight to ten each. Twenty-seven-foot ceilings. Thirty-six hundred square feet. Your ceremony, *her* ceremony, will be up on the balcony *there*; you exit through the rotunda *there*; have your drinks and music in the Odeon Room next-*door*; reenter through the side rotunda *here*. And *voilà.*" He knelt to fold back a corner of the rug, revealing a shiny triangle of parquet dance floor. "The room has been transformed.

Tables set and decorated, buffet dinner, full orchestra, swing dancing. The works."

"And the vows and rings and all that—"

"Once again." With excruciating patience, he directed the flow with both hands: "Ceremony's on the balcony. Processional up, recessional down and out the door. Guests following ushers, ushers following family, family following you. Her. Chairs start out theater-style *there*, and when you reenter they're banquet-style *here*."

"Around five-foot rounders."

"Five-foot rounds." The young man's lips moved in something of a smile. "That's my recommendation, sir. You could try fifty-fours, but you're going to lose your elbow room."

"Fifty-four inchers."

"If you will."

Oscar surveyed the site, hands on hips, faking competence. "Can we get some pilasters in here?"

"That would be rather difficult, sir."

"Fine, fine. But I'm going to need some florals." He bobbed his head as if counting something. "And plenty of forks."

"Flowers, of course, are up to you. We can put you in contact with our hotel florist if you would like."

Oscar stuck up a hand. "No need."

"And"—there was a snicker in his voice—"I wouldn't worry about forks."

"Well, you say that now."

"Sir."

"Yes."

"I am afraid that I'm going to need to know the participants." His stance had turned stiffly professional: arms refolded, loafers apart.

"I told you. Two-twenty."

"Not the number of guests. The name of the bride."

"I can't reveal that."

"Then the groom. We simply must have a name."

"I can't give you a name."

"Then I cannot facilitate your event. The hotel," he declared, hairy chin aimed at the ceiling, "takes a great deal of pride in designing weddings on an individual basis. We would be pleased to accommodate all your wedding needs and site-specific requests, but in order to do so effectively I absolutely must insist—"

Which was too bad, Oscar thought as he left the Pegasus Room, almost turned into the Jade Room, descended the stairs before the Emperor Room and passed the men's room and exited through a different entrance to the gassy honks and marching droves of midtown. He was just starting to learn a thing or two.

"Marco?"

"What's up."

"Sorry I'm late."

"Definitely."

Marco wore a baseball cap—but a fashionable one, she noted, without a team name or animal logo.

His *dressy* cap, as evidenced by the taut designer shirt and khakis that rose, as he did, from the table. He motioned her into a chair. He was younger than she'd expected, although not necessarily too young. The keen eyes of a go-getter. The swollen arms of a gym-goer. There would be days, she persuaded herself, when he wouldn't wear the stupid cap.

"So you're Lauren."

"And you're Marco."

"Definitely." He was looking her over. "Damn."

Several Japanese men in headbands behind the sushi bar had hollered and bowed to her when she entered, and she bowed back to them now, causing them to bow again. After six years of the columns, she couldn't help noticing silly themes and garish motifs everywhere she went. Restaurants dressed themselves in gimmickry, their staff and menus ordered to keep up the act. Whole cities rallied around slogans; entire countries trussed up to entertain guests. Life was an overplanned wedding of things. A lunch date was nothing but practiced lines and costumed procedures, a klutzy first dance in public. Marco was staring.

"Damn," he said again. "I didn't expect you to be so—to be honest, I didn't think you'd be so good-looking."

"Thanks." She glanced down self-consciously at her bright yellow skirt and over to the two men at the next table, who stopped surveying her legs.

"No, definitely. Because you're a writer, right?"

"Right."

"Me too."

"Of course. Becky told me."

"And I get that all the time."

She frowned. "Get what."

"You know. About not expecting it."

"Expecting what."

"Just about me." He grinned sheepishly, as if she were pressing him on a point. "Being good-looking."

"Oh."

"But I want to be honest with you about something. All right?" He put a hand to his chest. "That's me. I'm going to be honest."

"Shoot."

He smiled again, a perfect piano of teeth. "I've never read your thing."

"Oh, please."

"Your magazine thing. About parties and whatnot."

"Weddings. Who cares. Actually, I'm relieved." Truly, it was better that way. More than once she'd been set up with imposters who turned out to be already engaged and interested only in her writing up their occasions. One guy even beckoned to the next booth, where his fiancée had been hiding, to have her gush and plead by his side. Marco was some kind of writer; that was bad enough. At least he wouldn't be a pest.

He examined the specials on the menu. His mouth twitched to sound out the names. He was unarguably good-looking, with a deep tan, dark eyes—and the jiggling knee, she noticed, of a boy trapped in study hall. She forced her mind back open. Boyish was good. Energy was good. Even bloated egotism had its strengths. He was probably one of those men who made bench-pressing sounds during sex, self-interested sounds—but she made herself take that back. Sounds were good. Sex was good.

"So what sort of writing do you do?" she asked.

"Becky must have told me, but I—"

"Screenplays." He snapped his fingers as he talked. "Yep. Got a screenplay going right now. But I'll write anything. Definitely. You know how it is."

"Definitely."

"And I tend bar. To make rent, know what I'm saying. Pay my dues and whatnot."

"Which bar?"

"Lowlight, down on Sixth. That's where I saw Becky."

"Ah."

So Becky had asked the bartender. She had pushed Lauren's unlisted number across a beer-puddled counter and ordered a date for her friend. Love on the rocks. Desperation, straight up. Lauren was mortified for a minute, then let it go. At least she hadn't made it a double.

"My main thing is this screenplay," Marco was saying. He patted his chest again. "That's my baby, yo." For a while he spoke of the script and its backers. Probable backers. Potential backers. He explained it with reference to other movies: a *Schindler's List* for Latinos; *Die Hard* meets *La Bamba* only without all the songs. He went on, with the same finger-popping enthusiasm, to plug his family. Like the Waltons, apparently, but Puerto Rican. His mom was Mother Teresa meets Julia Child. As he smiled and talked and smiled, she worked to imagine life with Marco. Mobile phone calls from the bar at two in the morning. Pseudomeetings with so-called producers at three. He did have exceptional teeth, she thought. Potential backers. He said *mira* instead of *uh*—there, he'd said it again—which she liked.

His knee ticked off the time as they ordered and ate their sushi. He described his five sisters, his next hot screenplay; his hot sisters, his next five screenplays. Lauren was proud of her skill with chopsticks— not cocky, no, but determined—and concentrated on bettering her technique with a dastardly pile of leftover rice. Suddenly he asked of her family with the same magnanimous gesture that he had used to seat her two hours earlier.

They were country folks in the country; there wasn't much to tell. Still, he seemed interested, so she let go her chopsticks and tried to loosen up. Her father had run a car and tractor repair shop while her mother ran the home, until he'd run off when Lauren was ten with a hairdresser from Indian Hills. An older brother was married in Idaho Falls, an older sister a veterinarian in Pocatello, while her mother hadn't budged from their sleepy hometown of Paris. Lauren had graduated from Boise State with a double major in French and journalism and wrote freelance for a year before striking out for Manhattan. But she still had pangs for where she was from, for the scraggly Blackfoot Mountains, the churning curve of the cold Snake River. The light-brown smell of the dock on Bear Lake. In fact, in her weaker moments of urban defeat she had even thought of—

"But you must have known people in the biz," he interrupted.

"The tractor biz?"

"The magazine biz. In New York."

"Well, just Becky. She edits fashion for the magazine. We were on the college paper together. Becky's from Wyoming, and moved out to Brooklyn the year before I came east. She was the one who told me to try out for their weddings column."

"No—*names*, I'm saying." His eyes had gone a shade darker. "Must've had a few names."

"I'd written a lot of pieces by then. I'd had *editors*. Is that what you—"

"Connections. You know."

She sipped her green tea. So he wanted the apology. *I don't deserve to be famous. You deserve to be famous. Anyone can be famous, given the right connections—a few names—and it really should have been you.* She ought not to go on dates with writers. Was Bill a writer? No, Bill was a doctor. Bill, doctor. Doctor's bill: she could remember that. What was Chris? Chris was dinner. Christmas dinner. But first she would see this through with Marco.

"Have you done any magazine writing?" she asked mildly.

"Bet."

"What kind?"

"All kinds. Slice of life." He made a slicing motion with his hand. "Got a few ideas."

"Do you? That must be nice. I feel like I haven't had an idea in —"

"Here we go." He had unfolded a piece of paper. "First idea. A column on guys."

"What is this?"

"It's a column on guys. *Mira*, I go around with my boys and get them to give me the inside dope on their feelings and whatnot. Things we don't tell the girls, know what I'm saying. Kind of a 'Dear Abby' meets 'Penthouse Forum.' Hold up." Snap. "Got another one." Snap, snap. "This'd be more of a diary. Single guy in New York. Think Anne Frank meets —"

"Wait a minute. Is this a pitch?"

He lowered the paper. Toyed with another smile. "You mean am I hitting on you?"

"I mean a pitch. That's why you're here, isn't it. To get yourself into the magazine."

He adjusted his baseball cap, looking around. "Naw, see —"

"Well, let me give *you* a pitch, Marco." She stood up. Knocked back her chair. "Think *The Goodbye Girl* meets *The Lonely Guy*. Can you picture it? Kind of a *My Dinner with André* without André." She halted to explain: "I'm André."

"I'm sorry, André. Lauren." He stuffed the paper away. "Sit down. Honestly." He gave her the teeth. "*I'm* meets *sorry.*"

"No, it doesn't. It actually doesn't, in this case." She walked backward to the door. "Screw meets you, though." The whole restaurant was looking, nobody bowing or even flinching. She pulled at the door and struggled out to the sidewalk, informing him as it closed: "I have a date to get to."

The elevator beeped upward, conking his eardrums, nearing the top of the tallest building in New York. He hadn't visited the World Trade Center since his mother had brought him at eight years old, and a longing for that afternoon, a grasp at her wispy memory, might have dampened his thoughts if he weren't picturing Lauren and where she might be. Hidden in her neighborhood. Squeezed on a subway somewhere. On newsstands all over; but that was no help. He would call her. He would never call her. He was too nervous, too awkward, too large to go out on a limb. Too busy, in any case, with a wedding to plan. Five months and counting. Fourteen, thirteen, twelve floors to go.

The wedding coordinator was a soprano woman in a nautical scarf and blazer. She led him on a tour of the skytop restaurant and positioned him before the famous Windows on the World. He couldn't help goggling at the sight in all directions, the setting sun behind New Jersey making silver of the Hudson

River, gold of all the buildings, humble for once, at his feet.

"You see the advantage," she whined behind his shoulder, "of height."

Seated on the couch in her office, he inspected the promotional photographs that hung on the walls—the sparkling view at night, a Jewish couple stomping a glass, a white wedding of white people being served by nonwhite people in tuxes and tails—as she peppered him with questions and marked down his answers in triplicate. He gave his own name as the groom. Invented the first name of a bride. "Five hundred," he announced when asked about guests, and was relieved when she nodded at the number. He should have thought of this before. But then she stopped writing. Smoothed her scarf.

"Now," she said. "To price."

"To price," he agreed. It sounded like a toast. He imitated the apprehensive sigh of a groom.

"Without the sales tax and our service charge of twenty-two percent, and before incidentals, including breakage and overtime, the cost will be in the neighborhood." She was watching him. "Of four hundred."

"Four hundred dollars?"

"Is that beyond your budget?"

"Oh, I don't have a budget. You see"—he paused in his delivery, lifted a hand— "money is no object."

"I see."

"But I have to say, that's a lot less than I'd expected."

"Splendid." She wrote something down. "Multiplied by five hundred, plus tax and service and incidentals . . . well, you can do the math. Now I'm sure the bride—was it Lara?—will want to come by and see the site for herself. If I know brides. And I do."

"By five hundred?"

She checked the form. "I'm certain that you said five hundred guests."

"And I'm certain you said four hundred dollars."

"A person."

He looked from the woman to a picture of the view to the actual view out the window, then back to her. He closed his mouth. "Of course. That's right. That's more like it. A person. So, times five hundred."

"Is that beyond y—"

"No, no. Not at all. As I said, money"—but he couldn't finish. Two hundred thousand dollars. Plus a forty-thousand-dollar service charge. Seventeen thousand dollars in sales tax. *I don't give a flying fuck about the financials*, Dawn had sprayed at him when he'd tried to get a sense of budgetary constraints. Which was probably for the best, he thought queasily, as he had just spent a quarter-million dollars.

"Splendid," the woman said again, less convincingly. "Now, where is our bride?"

"What's that?"

"The bride."

"Oh. She's, um, around. She just had a hectic day."

"Well, I would love to get her in, maybe sometime next week, to discuss details."

"You can discuss all the details with me."

"To be sure. But trust me." She lifted a finger. "The bride always needs to be kept fully—"

"Not this one."

"I see." She forged a smile. "And you're certain that she wants to pay for everything in advance."

"That's what she told me."

"And that I should contact you from this point on."

"Yup."

"How . . . modern."

"That's us."

When she had taken Dawn's credit card and left to retrieve a booklet of decorative suggestions, Oscar turned to the window. From such a height a city appears perfectly reasonable: a basic bar graph of ambition and achievement, a never-ending series of vertical attempts at things.

She was around, he thought. She just had a hectic day.

Bill turned out to be more or less as advertised. Husband material, as Kara had assured her, if a bit frayed at his edges. Snow on the roof, to use Kara's term: as a hairstylist, she tended to notice that first. Cardigan on the weekend. Ring on the finger, Lauren saw when he waved at her from the back of the coffee shop. But that was the right hand, not the left, and a chunky red stone the size of a Jolly Rancher.

"Harvard," he said when she asked him about it a few minutes later. "I don't know why I wear it anymore," he said, twisting the ring. "I don't think I can get the confounded thing off."

She noticed that his sweater advertised Harvard as well, and she pictured him writhing before a chest of drawers, unable to get that confounded thing off either. Having written so often of rings and the cuts and weights of stones, she knew all too much about them. They were ovals, they were pears, they were emeralds and baguettes, marquises and round brilliants. Their table facets gleamed above the crown and in the center of the girdle unless flaws in the culet or pavilion lowered the grade of clarity below VS2. She could recite the four Cs of diamond selection: color, cut, clarity, and cost. No, carat. Cost or carat? She had forgotten the fourth C—this was ridiculous—and suddenly that cheered her up. She smiled at Bill. Who cared about the last C? There was a gap in her jammed head, letting in light. She breathed more easily. Capable, it turned out, of forgetting her job.

"Now, your job," said Bill. "At the magazine. This is something you wish to continue."

"I think so. Actually, no. Not forever."

"Until you get married." When he smiled, his face wrinkled all the way to his ears.

"Could be," she said. "I'd also like to try and write a book."

"Ahhh." He was disappointed. "A book."

"That's the dream, anyway."

"Once upon a time," he said, "I too thought of writing a book."

"Is that right?"

"I would take a summer off from my practice and become an author. I was sure of it."

"A whole summer, huh."

"I write constantly, of course. Prescriptions, letters, notes. Hundreds of words a day, when you add them all up. I may be no Kirk Connolly, my dear, but I am certainly capable of spinning a yarn. So I thought I'd dash one off. I even had the typewriter cleaned and repaired. Back in my day," he said, "we used typewriters."

"Ha." She wondered when his day might have been. A quick search for a year engraved on the ring was foiled by his pinky. "So what happened?"

"I simply couldn't spare the time."

"Too bad."

"And my back went out."

"Ah."

He signaled to a waitress behind the counter—a *barista*, they were called here—who was locked in a struggle with a machine that emitted the shriek of a wounded jaguar. Posters on the wall provided analyses of roasting techniques and the climate of Sumatra. Employees wore mug-shaped lapel pins that identified them as Java Joe and Decaf Diedre. Lauren swooned. The invitations would be coffee-colored. The dress made of burlap. Bean pods in the bouquet. The cake—

"Dear?"

This snapped her back. *Dear?*

"Are you all right?"

"Fine. Sorry. I'm fine." She pulled her chair closer to the table. "So where were we?"

But they were nowhere. They were at the very beginning. They each ordered a cappuccino, and he remarked on that common ground. They happened to be wearing similar wristwatches, and he made much of that as well. They talked gropingly of Kara, and Bill claimed to have been nicked by her scissors on the same ear as Laura.

"Lauren," she corrected him.

He apologized. "I'm afraid I'm quite the idiot when it comes to names."

"But how could that be? You went to *Hartford*," she joked.

"Harvard," he said.

They stirred and sipped their drinks, wiped their lips. Cappuccino was not an ideal choice for a first date, she realized; but it was all part of the challenge of her day-long triathlon. She had scored well in the chopstick competition with Marco. She would have to order something harder—tacos, maybe, or cotton candy—with Chris. "And you're a doctor," she tried again with Bill.

"A podiatrist, yes."

"Forgive me: is that—kids?"

"Could be." He crinkled another smile. "Should they have foot problems."

This, she thought, was the hard part. There was a hard part, and then it got easier. She strove to picture life with Bill: black-tie reunions in Cambridge, the day-to-day of it in New York. Public television, she guessed, with the volume turned down. Walking shoes, driving gloves: the supple equipment of the old at heart. A full-color diagram of feet on the bathroom wall. A masterful foot rub in bed. She smiled involuntarily: she loved foot rubs. His eyes bent back at her.

"I'm enjoying myself," he stated.

"You are?"

"Don't be so surprised. You're a heck of a girl." He sucked at the top of his foam. "I would like to give you my number." He dug into the pocket of his slacks and handed her a pen that bore his address and telephone number above the block-lettered motto: LIFE IS A JOURNEY, ONE FOOT AT A TIME.

"Hey. Thanks."

His expression turned grave. "I must tell you, dear, that I am in the process of getting over something."

She nodded, matching his solemnity. A divorce, she thought. A death. A heel spur.

"It lasted four years, and her name was Leanne. She was a doctor as well. Columbia."

A Colombian doctor, she almost said, maintaining her frown.

"And you."

"Me? Oh, me." This was the worst part, she thought: the patient history. "Well, I've had a few boyfriends," she said. She rolled the pen back and forth on the table between them. "It's not that I haven't dated."

"Mmm."

"But it's been a while now. I've been busy. Because of the column."

"Mmm."

"So no one recently."

He folded his hands. "Career," he diagnosed, "is extremely important to you."

"My career? Well, yes and no."

"Exclusively important."

"Not exclusively, no." Her defensiveness rose with the noise of frothing across the room. She felt as if she were trying to sublet him an apartment, to sell him a used car.

"And you would like children."

"Children? Yes." And there it was, she thought: the problem with the plumbing, the rattle under the hood. "In time," she put in. "No hurry. But eventually, sure, I want kids."

What she wanted was someone to make her laugh. It came to her in the last swallow of her cappuccino: that was all she needed, a good laugh. She'd cackled while attempting to waltz on that stupid plank, to come up with excuses to speak softly in Oscar's ear, to press her cheek to his good heavy chin. But he was getting married. She turned her thoughts with caffeinated hopefulness to Chris. He might make her laugh. A downstairs neighbor in her building had arranged that one. Chris was a graduate student in something; grad students could be funny. Theology, Lauren remembered. She bit her lip and looked away.

She wanted something better, someone bigger than all this. Someone chuckling above it, the way she was. The world can be divided into two types of men, those you tried to settle and those you settled for; and Lauren wanted neither. Not Marco and all the Marcos, that rowdy tribe of eternal boys who continued to sport high-top sneakers in the hope of being yanked out of adulthood and into a game. And not Bill, from the other camp: a camp of birdwatchers and robe wearers, of back trouble and colon concerns that drove men rapidly over the hill. She had the sudden urge to blurt out, *Well, thanks for your time, Bill. I'll let you know.* To kiss him hard on his liverish lips. To leap atop the counter and lead the café in a rollicking singalong, an anthem of foot care and feet. But there were no songs about feet. There was nothing.

Lunch and coffee and so far nothing.

His studio apartment was as tight a fit as any on the Upper West Side, rendered habitable only by his stringent attention to order. The kitchen also served as the dining or living room, depending on whether the chair was pushed into or beside the table. Opening the oven door revealed his television (he never baked), and by zippering his covers into a cushion case each morning he created a second seat. The only recent addition to his scrupulous floor plan was an object shaped like a coffee table and draped with a tablecloth. If it weren't for his ever-present heap of weekend reading, the room might even be roomy.

He turned on his lamp and spread the latest boxed and bagged assortment across his futon in order of the hopeful authors' last names. He restacked them into fiction and nonfiction: two blocks of submissions, a half dozen in each. These were Dawn's manuscripts, to be read and rejected by his letters, signed with her signature, by Monday. This was his Saturday night, ten years of Saturday nights in a row. Sunday night too, to judge from the height of the pillars. But not this weekend. He lifted and removed the manuscripts to the floor, turned and whisked the tablecloth off his complete set of back issues of the magazine.

He had ordered them through the publicity department, arranged payment as part of a marketing budget, and had them shipped to his home by persuading the mailroom that it was a West Side studio of Dawn's. There were nearly a hundred of them, dating back almost a decade to when cover models wore tube tops and tans. He reached for the top few copies, sat, and plunked them on his lap. He fluttered the perfumed pages until he located the table of contents. Read her name aloud. Then he hurried past the photos of shoes and quizzes on orgasm until he found her monthly dispatch on the subject of other people's luck.

RaShelle Jackson, 29, met Keith
Levine, 30, where she expected to meet
her doom: on line to bungee-jump off a

ledge of Bryce Canyon in southern Utah. After talking and stalling for the better part of an hour, the two exchanged kisses of encouragement and assurances of safety and watched each other leap off into the abyss. And on a recent Saturday afternoon in a lodge beside the same canyon, they stood before an audience of eighty friends and family and did essentially the same thing.

Jay Veltman, 33, did not expect Sabina Clifton, 28, to be pretty. "It was a chat room relationship. We only knew each other's screen names," he recalls. "Even our words were mushed and abbreviated: 'tx' and 'pls' and 'lol.' I guess I expected her to look, I don't know. Mushy. Short." But what started in casual lowercase ended up headlining a weekend of computer-based marital festivities at the couple's new home in Seattle, complete with virtual reality displays of their first date and CD ROMs bearing their vows.

He was immersed in last summer's story of Edwin Sexton III and Amy Elizabeth Simms—of their meeting on the college crew team, their wedding in a boathouse, their exit from the ceremony under a wooden canopy of oars held aloft—when the phone rang. He jumped. The crack of Dawn. He looked guiltily at the neglected manuscripts before picking up the phone.

"Hello, Dawn Bo— Oops. Hello."

"Hi. Oscar?"

"This is Oscar."

"Oh. Good. It's Lauren. LaRose."

"It *is*?" His voice escalated wildly. "How are *you?*"

"Fine."

She sounded different. Farther away, that was all. Hopelessly far away.

"Just thought I'd call," she said briskly. "You were listed. And I had a minute. Found myself between a couple of things. Rocks, hard places, all kinds of things."

"You're talking very fast. Are you okay?"

"Fine, fine, fine. I just had way too much coffee."

"Are you at a wedding?" He sat down on the manuscripts, breaking a couple of the boxes. "It sounds like you're on a cell phone."

"Pay phone. And you were listed. So I just thought: Hey."

"Sure," he said. "Hey."

"Listen, I'd better get going. I just wanted to ask you if our deal was still on."

"The deal? Absolutely. You want me to look at a column?"

"I could use you, yes."

"Not a problem," he said. "Oh, you know what? I got a place today."

"You're moving?"

"What? No. A place. For the wedding. Like you said."

"Ah, right," she said. "The wedding."

"Thanks for the advice; it was a huge help. I'd love to get your input on ministers at some point. You said that's next."

"Well, a deal's a deal."

"Great."

"I didn't hear that. Oscar? I think my quarter's running out."

"I just said *great.*"

"Ah."

"So go ahead and fax the article to me at work. I'll give you the number."

"Just a sec. Let me look for a pen. I never have a pen."

"I get to the office early, so no one will see it but me. What's it about? Where was the wedding?"

"You really want to know?"

"Of course I do." He looked over the salad of open magazines on his couch. "You may not know this"—he switched to Maggi's voice—"but I'm like the most humongous fan of 'Aisle of White.'"

She giggled. "Ohmygod."

"Do you have a pen?" he asked her. "I'll give you the fax number."

There was an odd sound in her throat. "Do I ever."

She sat at the bar, full on the free pistachios. She would have left by then—the guy was a good hour late—if it weren't for a sporty desire to finish the triathlon. The trilling of Italian music had started over,

*O Sole Mio*ing on a relentless loop. It was a romantic restaurant, a first-date factory. She watched all the couples trading antipasti, sharing cannolli, splitting the check. Two stools away, a black-haired woman appeared to have been stood up as well. From time to time she spun toward Lauren and shot her a look of suffering camaraderie. *"Men,"* Lauren finally sighed at her, hamming it up. The woman rotated away as if offended.

Twenty minutes went by before she rotated back. "You're not Lauren."

"Excuse me? I'm Lauren."

"Shoot." She gave a grin. Brushed her hair from her eyes. "I'm Chris."

"You're—no you're not."

She stuck out a hand. "Great first impression, huh? Sorry about that. I thought I heard you say something about a man."

"I did." Chris's hand was tender and cool after the apelike mitts of the men. "I think I just said *men*."

"I thought so. Why?"

"Why men?"

"Yeah."

"Why not?" Lauren tried to laugh. "No, it's just. Uh."

"You didn't think—"

"I didn't know."

"Wait. You're serious. This is unbelievable. Svenja didn't say anything? She didn't *describe* me? She didn't happen to mention the first freaking thing about me?"

"I don't really know Svenja," Lauren hurried to explain. "She lives a floor below me. I did know that *she's* a woman. I mean, I knew *she* was—"

"—gay."

"Right. She must have just used your name. No pronouns. And I assumed, when she offered to set me up with someone, that she knew I was, you know—"

"—not."

"That's the word."

They sat for a while, not spinning on their stools.

"I don't freaking believe this."

"I know. Me neither."

"I'm going to kill her," Chris said.

"I don't even know her."

"Then you can help."

They were seated by the window. A waiter lit their candle, the wax molded to resemble Italy with a wick at the top of the boot. They ordered a carafe of the house Chianti. Chris had read and liked Lauren's column on a lesbian wedding in Hawaii, a gourmet luau aboard a giant bamboo raft, and wondered aloud how guests had been able to go to the bathroom. This sent Lauren into a lecture on the mathematics of portable toilets: each capable of a hundred and twenty-five uses, divided by the average human need of once every three hours, rounded up by the intake of alcohol and the risk of motion sickness to a sum of four Porta Potties at the four corners of the craft off the coast of Lanai. Math was the skeleton of a wedding, she philosophized. From there it was fleshed out with personality, clothed in style.

But Chris didn't care much for weddings. She had dated men through college in Toronto before she met the right woman and applied to the Union Theological Seminary in Manhattan to be with her. They moved into a charming apartment on a cute block seven months ago. Chris was left for a pottery teacher six months after that.

"Brutal," she recalled. "Two-bedroom on Twenty-Fourth Street. Hardwood floors. Broke my heart."

"*Women,*" said Lauren, and they laughed at that.

"Which brings me here." Chris looked up through a lock of hair. "What's your story."

"Mine? I don't have a story. I tell other people's stories."

"Tell me yours."

"I literally don't have one."

"So tell me why not."

She traced the stem of her glass. "That's the question, isn't it."

"It's because you don't let them run a picture of you in the magazine."

"Ha. Thanks. But that's not why. I think it has more to do with what they *do* run in the magazine. I think it's because the rest of the human race is so busy meeting each other in my first paragraph, living together in my second paragraph, and slipping on rings in time for me to credit the caterer and paint the setting that I don't have time to try it myself. No time: that's the reason." She thought for a moment. Shook her head. "That's not the reason. It's because I have too *much* time. See, I'm

way too picky. Because if I'm not—and here's the real
problem—then I'm not picky *enough*."

"You have no idea, do you."

"Not a clue," she said. "I know how people meet.
That's my subject. Every month. But I don't have the
foggiest notion why they don't." She looked out the
window. A dog was peeing on the leg of an occupied
baby carriage as their owners waited to push and pull
them across the street. "It's this place," she said. "This
place is what's wrong."

"We could go somewhere else."

"No, I mean—"

"I could take you to *my* kind of place." Her face
glowed closer in the candlelight.

"Oh, I don't think so. Just because I've run
through all the heterosexual options in the greater
metropolitan area is no reason to start hurling myself
at women." She chewed a piece of bread. "This city is
the problem. It's depressing. You know, Chris. Look
around."

She looked around. "What."

"It's all couples. All over the place. Couple after
couple after couple. Gay and straight, brown and
pink, black and blue. There's one. There's another one.
I'm looking for a table, a single table, without a couple. Looking, looking. These people are together: you
can tell because they're not talking."

"Don't point."

"They're everywhere. Ex-professors and elevator
operators, violin teachers and skateboarders: they all

somehow find each other. It's a miracle. Two by two, hand in hand, block after block. It's like being trapped on Noah's Ark. You should know about this. You must study Noah's Ark."

"My dissertation has more to do with lesbian priesthood over the course of European hist—"

"Then let me tell you something, Chris. About single men. Because you've probably forgotten."

"I haven't forg—"

"They don't exist. That's the trick. You meet someone, and he's taken. You see somebody who happens to be alone and available, and it turns out he's not. You finally get *really* lucky and wind up with some great guy someplace you'd never expect to find him, and he's engaged."

"You met someone?"

"The ark is filling up fast. That's all I'm saying. And I don't have a seat."

"Oh yeah?" said Chris. "Well, I don't have an *ark*."

The waiter who brought their food was attractive enough, with the pointed face and bushy eyebrows of a fox. The wedding band of a husband, Lauren saw as he set down her pasta. He gave her a spoon and a long beady look before skulking back across the restaurant and peeping at her from there.

"How old are you?" Chris asked.

"Thirty-two," she said. "What about you?"

"Same."

"Ha. See?"

"See what?"

Lauren nodded profoundly. "It gets harder, doesn't it."

"It's always hard."

"Not this hard." She planted her fork in her tagliatelli for emphasis. "And I'll tell you why."

"This ought to be good."

"It's not what you think. It's not that we haven't been active or interesting enough. As a matter of fact, we're at a distinct disadvantage because we *have*. By the time you get past thirty you've done too much. You know too much. I sit there on all these dates, and I just—*know* too *much*." She watched the ducking and flaring of the candle. "I know exactly who these guys are, and who I am, and I know the impossible distance between the two. And I know that my twentysomething ability to be a pretty, sticky blob—shaped by whoever squeezes me, sticking to whoever touches me—ended at about age twenty-nine. I've hardened. Haven't you? We're grown-ups, now, with our own built-up lives and broken-down ideas, and it's virtually impossible to find the one person who's going to match up with all our jagged edges."

"You don't *match* with people," said Chris. "You fall in love with them."

"Do you?"

"You do. You get swept off your feet. Carried away. By chance. By surprise."

"Is that what they teach you in divinity school?"

"That," she said, "is *exactly* what they teach you in divinity school."

A look of concern crossed Lauren's face. "Would you hold my hand?"

"I thought we'd been over this."

"Look over there. Our waiter's giving me the eye."

He stood in his gondolier's outfit before a mural of the Tuscan countryside, his furry eyebrows raised.

"He's giving you the whole face," said Chris. She reached around the bread basket to grab Lauren by the palm.

"Excellent."

"Keep talking. Look at me and say something, Lauren. And try not to get turned on."

"Oh, don't worry."

"I'm not worried," she said. "You look a little worried, though."

"I'm not."

"Little unsure of yourself. Little tempted."

"Cut it out."

They broke down laughing.

"Is he still watching?"

"He's still watching. Wait, he's crying," Lauren narrated. "He's sobbing."

"No he's not."

"My God, he's masturbating."

"Lauren."

They laughed harder, dabbing at their eyes with their free hands.

"Keep talking."

"Right, keep talking." Lauren tried to look serious.
"What were we talking about?"

"You were telling me about your love life."

"No, I wasn't. You were telling me about divinity
school."

"Same difference."

"Hey, thanks a lot."

"Well, think about it. There are parallels."

She thought about it. "You're going to tell me that
it just takes faith."

"Bingo."

"Ha. I'd call it a miracle."

"Don't knock miracles," said Chris, her hand tight-
ening for a moment before letting her go.

The Minister

Inside Hangar 2 at the McConnell Air Force Base in Wichita, Kansas, a launch of the amorous variety was taking place. The B-1B Lancer was in position to roll out and head for the skies; but its wings were festooned with carnations, its tail number repainted with "Anthony & Trish." Model airplanes hung from the high metal ceiling. Guests with seating cards shaped like boarding passes found their chairs at a banquet table that stretched the length of the cement floor. The bride and groom were on their way, descending toward the tarmac in the hot-air balloon where they'd spoken their vows.

"This is the perfect way for Trisha and Tony to get married," said Kathleen Misrahi, 32, the bride's maid of honor and a fellow flight attendant from nearby Chadwick, Missouri. "Their life together is just taking off."

After training as a fighter pilot at McConnell and working as a commercial pilot for Delta Airlines, Anthony Cardillo, 38, knew very well how to break out of a holding pattern, to recognize a sunny window of opportunity and make the most of it. "Trish and I had been dating for seven years," he explained, "and it was time to land this thing." So toward the end of a twelve-and-a-half-hour flight from Washington to Johannesburg, once the customs forms were distributed and the headphones collected, Anthony switched on his captain's mike and made the announcement. "Flight attendants, please prepare the cabin for landing," he said. "And Trisha Jakimczyk, prepare to be mine."

*H*e finished reading over his edits and fed the article back into the fax machine, standing alone in the slowly warming hall. In a matter of minutes the elevators would thrum to life. The receptionist would arrive and install herself between a full Diet

Coke can and a package of press-on nails, each to be emptied over the course of the morning. The snippy girls from paperbacks would show up with wet hair, the contract lawyer with her knock-knock jokes, the head of the design department with a fresh pierce in his tongue. Oscar felt a kind of claustrophobic affection for these people, for this sunlit section of the eleventh floor. On the brink of the day he was awash with an unfamiliar feeling: the sense that he'd worked here long ago and had survived it, already moved on and safely away. It must have been the wedding columns that he'd devoured over the last few weeks, the mountain of magazines reduced to a flat splay, that had left him with this notion of a neat life story, with the ability to look back to the present with the pride of a veteran. He had settled down, fallen in love. Strange to think of what he'd put up with, and how long he'd put up with it, before he had gotten lucky enough to leave.

"Vicar," said Carl. "Clergyman."

He gave a grunt over his shoulder.

"Preacher, pastor, chaplain, priest."

"What was after pastor?"

"Chaplain."

"As in Charlie?"

"As in parson. As in deacon. Ecclesiastic."

Oscar wrestled with the top edge of the window, towering above the man at his desk. "I'll have this in a minute, Carl. Go ahead. I'm listening."

"Padre. Father. Reverend. Rabbi." Carl nosed closer to the page of the thesaurus that he'd propped beside his plate and silverware. "Abbé, evangelist, and revivalist."

"That's it?"

"That's the extent of it. No luck up there, eh." He tined and sliced his salmon, inserted a morsel into his mouth.

"I may have budged it. Hold on. Rrrr." Oscar pulled downward with the last of his strength and the window snapped open. "Whew." He descended from his tiptoes. "Fresh air."

"Hurrah for height."

"That was worse than yesterday," he said. "You may want to have maintenance come check that out." He watched Carl pat his mouth with the napkin that hung from his collar. "You're the only person I know who actually sets a table at his desk for lunch."

"There is no reason, my boy, when faced with the daily blasphemy and common anarchy of life"—he conducted the sentence with his salad fork—"to lose all sense of decorum."

Even with the new breeze, there remained a fuggsy odor about the room, an old attic smell; although there were no sepia photos or dusty children's toys stored here, not a relic of a life to be seen. Only papers everywhere: five or six manuscripts on the desk, eight or ten on a file cabinet containing still more letters, chapters, and reams. Stubs of red pencil and red pencil marks were speckled about every square surface, encroaching on Carl as if he were in danger of being deleted himself.

"So what would be the difference," Oscar asked, indicating the thesaurus, "between a *padre* and a *father?*"

"*Padre*, I believe, would be the Spanish derivation of the Latin *pater*, or 'father.' Thus they are nomenclatural twins, geographically estranged."

"But which would you want at your wedding?"

"At my wedding? Well now. That would be impossible to say." Flustered, apparently, by the very conception of romance, he let the knife clash onto the rim of his plate. "Why do you inquire?"

"About ministers? Preachers? Just, um, wondering."

"You're not getting married, I trust."

"Oh no," Oscar laughed. "Is there anything else you need? Besides the window? I have to do something for Marion and get back to Dawn before her lunch."

"You've turned thirty."

"A year ago. Why?"

Carl clamped a hand to his chest. "*So thou through windows of thine age shalt see, despite of wrinkles, this thy golden time.* That's Shakespeare."

"So it is. I should really go see Marion and—"

"Permit me to guess the following," he said. "You do not have a girlfriend."

"As it happens, Carl, I don't."

"Hearken the trumpets. Batten the hatches." He

placed down his fork and folded his hands behind his head. The smell of his armpits crowded the office. "I, too, can recall turning thirty."

"Can you really?"

"Such are the milestones of a masculine life, the stumbling blocks that send you reeling into the thought that things may be passing you by. That women, indeed, may be passing you by. And to be certain, they are."

"Thanks for the talk, Carl."

"Yet there is work to be done. Men *work*, you see: it is our calling. Our vocation. From the Latin *vocatio*, a summons. Nose to the grindstone. Pedal to the metal, if you prefer. The world can be divided into workers and dozers. Dozers take romantic honeymoons from life, dancing and kissing it away. Workers work at it."

"Interesting."

"You, my young friend, are a worker." He carved off another triangle of salmon. "As am I."

A vision rose before Oscar, made more vivid by the sweatshop smell of the room. It was an image of thousands—no, millions—of workers, a worldwide crew of haggard men roped by neckties and lurching with briefcases on their way to nothing much, shuffling home to nothing at all. His father was there, having spent forty years running the Campbell family insurance business securely into the ground. Carl was there too, marching before the troops with his red pencil raised. For a moment Oscar saw himself among their legion, head and shoulders above them but with the same vacant gaze. But when he looked harder, to his relief, he was gone.

"There's just something about a handyman," Marion purred at his back.

Oscar tugged out the old cartridge, powdering his palms with indelible ink. He ripped the foil off the replacement and gave it the requisite back-and-forth shake before sliding it slowly into the copy machine. He was a top-notch surgeon heading a high-risk operation. A master defuser of bombs, steady-fingered with seconds to go. And then it occurred to him: Marion would know her. She knew everyone in publishing, her earring to the door of all print industry affairs.

"Do you know Lauren LaRose?" he asked without turning around.

"'Aisle of White'? Of course I know it. I told *you* about it."

"No, I'm ask—"

"Do I read it? Every woman in America reads that preposterous column. We can't help ourselves."

He closed the top of the printer and listened to it swallow and hum. "So you like it."

"No, I don't like it. It's irritating. It's idiotic. I *devour* it. I'm telling you, everyone does."

He tried to dust off his stained hands. "But you don't know her."

"Know who. La-La LaRose?"

"Lauren."

"Right, Lauren. No, I don't know her. Nobody knows her. Listen, is Dawn in? I have to ask her about the spring sales conference. Has she chosen a date?"

"The date. Right. She's, um, deciding today." He would have to decide that for her today. "She'll probably announce it at the four o'clock meeting."

"Can you get me some time with her before that?"

"Afraid not. She's about to leave for lunch."

Marion looked at the wall clock that hung beside her Tommy Gunn concert poster. "It's eleven-forty-five," she said. "What lunch?"

"Long lunch."

"What about after that?"

"She'll be gone until the meeting."

"I'll wait outside her office."

"You can't. I have authors coming in."

"You? Who's coming in to see *you*?"

"Printer's all set." He gave it a tap. "I'll see you at the meeting."

"What's this lunch, Oscar?"

"It's a meal," he said. "Like dinner, only smaller." He walked toward the door.

"Oscar."

"Honestly, I have to go. Dawn's leaving any second."

Her voice carried after him into the hall. "What the hell is going on around here?"

"White limo, west entrance, five minutes," he said as he steered himself into Dawn's office behind his clipboard. "The *Wildflowers* cover has been changed to matte. Your massage is switched to Tuesday. Tommy Gunn's touring with Aerosmith." He slid a piece of paper onto her desk.

"Touring?" She whirled toward him in her desk chair, brandishing a water bottle. "Better be back in time for sales conference."

"He'll be back."

"That's our lead nonfiction title for spring."

"He knows. I talked to his manager. What's our lead fiction title, by the way?"

Dawn stood, kicking her chair back against the wall. "Working on that."

"Have you decided on a date for sales conference? It's in New York this year. Marion has been pester—"

"Spring, Oscar. It's the spring sales conference."

"I know. But have you narrowed—"

"You narrow." She was putting on her frizzy white coat. The sight, from where he stood, was that of a woman grappling with a polar bear. "Pick a damn date, Oscar. Eenie meenie. You're holding up publicity. I'm late for lunch."

He noted the command, arched and dotted a question mark.

"And who's Hairsmith?"

"Who?" he asked.

"And what the hell's this?" She grabbed and held up the piece of paper.

"That's the breakdown on the wed— on the project," he said quietly, moving toward her. "Date and time are up top: March sixteenth, four-thirty. The prices are on the right. I thought it might be helpful for you to see it all spelled out."

"What did I tell you about this?"

"You said top secret."

"I said," she seethed, "to do it yourself."

"I am. I just thought—"

"Don't think, Oscar. I don't pay you to think. I pay you to assist me. If you want to start thinking, I'm going to start paying you less."

She was out of her office by the time the seesawing paper landed at his feet. He picked it up. Read it again. Five hundred friends, he thought, would be difficult to find.

With that, the place was his. She would be out with Gordy until midafternoon, making him ruler of the snowy kingdom, the duke of Dawn Books, and making her office available for his very first meetings with authors. Over the course of the week, he had rotated his Rolodex and copied into his binder the names and numbers of several spiritual best-sellers who ought to be able to handle a wedding. Who might even be able, given their otherworldly powers, to handle Dawn.

His one o'clock appointment was with the author of *Soul Survivor*, a Nigerian shaman who promptly emptied a leather sack of bones across Dawn's carpet to read Oscar's future. One-forty-five saw the sweeping entrance of the author of *The Souls of Your Feet*, a Danish healer who insisted on feeling Oscar's aura, clambering up on a chair to reach the top half. The creator of a spiritual diet book, *Filet of Soul,* led him through various breathing exercises and a lengthy monologue on the value of orange vegetables. Nor did his three o'clock appear much more promising: all smiles in her clownish makeup, windmilling the arms of her gauzy robe.

"But in terms of the ceremony," he finally interrupted. She had been describing her ability to channel the dead, a subject already exhaustively covered in the first chapter of *Soul Kiss.*

"Mmm. Your ceremony."

"Not my— Yes. Sorry. My ceremony. How do you see the—"

"I see," she began, rocking back and forth in the guest chair, "a death."

"Yikes. At the wedding?"

"Before the wedding," she said. "Many years before the wedding."

"See, this is the problem." He was feeling rather authoritative in Dawn's throne, his confidence cushioned by the white leather. "Maybe I didn't make myself clear on the phone." He swiveled to test the lateral action: smooth. "I need to find a minister. For a wedding."

"She's passed on."

"The minister? But I didn't have one. I was hoping you might be—"

"Cancer." The woman had closed her eyes.

"What?"

"Her death was caused by cancer. You were

young, very young. I see a number now. Nine. You were nine and you lived in, wait a minute . . . New Jersey. And you loved her." Her eyelids trembled. Her robe was unpleasantly transparent in the harsh light of the office. "And she loved you. She was, hold on a minute . . . your mother."

"Listen," he said quickly, feeling himself blush. "I'm not a big believer in this sort of thing. I had one of those Lucky Eight Balls when I was little, the kind you shake up and it gives you answers, and I have to tell you: it was wrong. All the time."

"You're an assistant," said the woman.

"Well, true."

"You assisted her when she was sick."

"My mother?"

"And you assist him whenever you're home."

"My father, you mean. I make the guy dinner. Tidy up a bit. I really don't think that constitut—"

"And you assist people now."

"That's my job, yes."

"Too many people. Or too much of *one* person." Her arms dangled outward from her sides like an old television antenna. "When you work too hard to help others," she said, "it can keep you from helping yourself."

"Good to know."

"From taking *chances,*" she added. "You have never taken a chance."

"I wonder if we could get back to the wedding." He tapped on his open binder. Looked at his watch.

"What I really need from you is a sense of how the ceremony might pro—"

"Ah!" She threw her arms in the air. "You have a fiancée."

"Eureka. I told you that."

"You're getting married."

"Yes. As I've said. Which is why I need a few specifics here. For example: how much would you charge to conduct, say, a half-hour ceremony? Keeping in mind that dinner's included."

"But there's a misunderstanding."

"There sure is," he said.

"Between you and your fiancée."

Already he hated the word *fiancée*. It sounded as if he were marrying into the French bourgeoisie, or indulging in something as exotic as a *flambé* or *ménage-à-trois*. He was suspicious of foreign languages, truth be told, having failed every one he attempted in high school and college. The frequent use of imported nouns by the wordsmiths of the wedding industry seemed a cultivated attempt to mask hidden fees.

"You must call her."

"Oh, I will. We talk all the time. We're fiancés. Fiancéd." He waved off her concern, almost knocking over Dawn's china cup of paper clips.

"Call her," she said again. She opened her eyes. "Right away."

"I don't think you understand."

"You have only a minute."

"You're serious," he said.

"Sooner or later, you will have to take a chance."

"And call her."

She gave a mystical smile. "For now," she said, "that will do."

He wiped the bone dust from Dawn's rug and the shoe smudges from her chair, escorted his guest to the elevators and returned to his desk. Grasped and let go of the phone. Dawn's message light was blinking maniacally, although he had collected and transcribed two sets of midday calls already. Three-fifty-one, according to the clock on his computer. The main number of the magazine was printed at the bottom of Lauren's fax. He'd fallen flat on the minister; he might as well call for her advice. After a quick breathing exercise, he picked up the receiver and dialed.

A receptionist patched him through to someone who rattled off instructions for the submission of wedding information. He broke in to explain that this was a personal call, whereupon he was informed that Ms. LaRose worked from home and the message would be delivered as soon as possible. As he hung up, he pictured her home: a bohemian loft, quill pens in ink wells, Persian cats on Persian rugs. He dialed in for the last batch of messages and set about transcribing and dividing them into unmentionables and no-longer-ignorables. He had deleted the last recorded plea and replaced the phone when it rang. His line. He breathed. Breathed. And hoisted it to his ear.

"Dawn Books."

"Oscar?"

"This is."

"It's Lauren."

"Hi. Great. Hello."

"I can't believe you called. I was just stopping home for a second before I have to head off again. Great Gatsby wedding in Sacramento. You barely caught me."

"Lucky me."

"Hey, thanks for your help on the Kansas column. I went by the office and read the new draft. It's perfect."

"It was easy," he said. "You're a very good writer."

"And you're a very good editor."

"Good," he said. "Good to hear. So . . . good." He was stuck.

"So don't tell me. You have a wedding question."

"What?"

"That's our deal. Don't be shy. It's the only reason anyone ever calls me. Concerns about the cake. Debates over the dress. Hit me."

"Um, sure. A wedding question." He opened his binder in a panic, riffled the pages to Ceremony. "What I wanted to ask—here it is. I need a minister."

"You don't have a minister? Didn't you ever go to church?"

"My dad's Jewish."

"Temple, then?"

"My mom was Christian."

"Ah. So the religion is up to you."

"I was afraid you were going to say that."

"No, that's good," she said. "That gives you all the options."

"I'm starting to hate all the options."

"Just pick and choose. I'll help you. I've got five minutes before I miss my plane."

If it's Judaism you're after, then schedule with care; for there's no marrying on the Sabbath or High Holy Days, nor during the seven weeks between Passover and Shavuot. The good news is that the ceremony's over in less than an hour. Hindu weddings, by contrast, stretch for days. If you're interfaith, think Unitarian. If you're into sake, consider Shinto. Muslim wives propose to their husbands; Catholic women are married by men. Sikh brides have their hands painted with henna. Hindu grooms get their feet washed by their in-laws. To Episcopalians marriage is a sacrament; to the Russian Orthodox it's a chance to wear crowns.

"What's she?" Lauren asked.

"She? Nothing. I don't know."

"You don't know your wife's religion?"

"She's not my wife."

"Apologies. Fiancée."

"No, what I'm trying to tell you"—but he couldn't tell her. Not a national magazine columnist, of all people. She would know Dawn's name, leak the secret, spread the word. He pounded softly on his forehead with a fist. "Do you want to have lunch?"

"What?"

Before he could repeat himself, it was Dawn. "Oscar." She marched past his desk. "Oscar. Get off the phone, Oscar. Get off. The phone."

"Gotta go," he said. "Staff meeting."

"I should run too. I have to get a cab to La Guardia."

"Right."

"So you have my number," she said.

"Actually, I don't."

"Terrific."

"Get. The *fuck*. Off the *phone*," Dawn yelled.

"What about, um, lunch?"

"Lunch sounds great. I'm back from California on Sunday."

"How's Monday?" He might have said Tuesday, he considered. Played it cooler; taken a day.

"Monday works for me." She could have hemmed and hawed about it, she thought. Kept him guessing. She would stand firmer on the choice of restaurants. "Wherever you want," she said.

He took the empty seat between Marion and Carl, nodded at the sales guys from six and the production staff from nine, and hunched forward to take minutes as Dawn began to speak. With angry raps on the conference room table, she instructed that the paper people use thinner stock. That authors be put up at motels instead of hotels. That Marion arrange for more book signings, as written-on copies were unreturnable by stores. Oscar transcribed her rantings and doodled in the margin the number "500." What had possessed him to utter such an unattainable sum? Where on earth would he find that many people who could stand her?

Dawn punched the table harder. Everyone jumped in their seats.

"Big news, people. Hot off the damn presses," she said. "You are looking. At the new. Publisher." She blew on her fingernails, buffed them against her blouse. "Of Kirk Connolly."

"*What?*" Marion gaped at her. "Not *the* Kirk Connolly. Not the thriller writer. The action movie blockbuster guy."

"What do I tell you people. I tell you to think big. Do you? No. But I think big. And when I think big. I think. Kirk. Connolly." She made the motion of plucking him out of the air and putting him in her pocket. "Gotcha."

A hubbub swept the table.

"I thought he was Random House," said someone from marketing.

"Putnam," corrected a woman from special sales.

"*Was* Putnam," said Dawn. "Now he's Dawn Books. Get it straight."

"And how, pray tell," Carl ventured, "did you entice the fellow?"

"You paid a *fortune*," Marion guessed. "How much, Dawn. Come on. Must have been a fortune."

Oscar was getting down the information, his head ducked close to the page. "And who's the agent on that?"

Dawn gave him a look that he felt through the top of his head. "Fox."

"Oh, Fox. Sure. Got it. And, um, what's the novel about?" he chirped, attempting to cover the moment.

"What's it about, he wants to know." She glared around at her staff. "What a goddamn question. What was the last novel about? What are all Kirk Connolly novels about? IRA terrorists, Palestinian plane bombings, arson, homicide, cyanide. Who the hell knows. Who cares? They're thrillers. They're about thrills. They're about"—she knocked again on the table— *"money."*

There was scattered applause, a few dry laughs.

"How did you get Fox to do it? It just doesn't make sense. You must have broken the bank. How much? Ballpark figure."

"Shut your trap, Marion. Other business."

She was pleased, Oscar could tell. Kirk Connolly was a bigger deal, a bigger name, than any in Dawn Books' history, and that made her a bigger deal and a bigger name than ever. She was flushed with the richness of the transaction, pink-cheeked above the pale collar of her shirt. This, he thought, was Dawn's religion: a faith in the arrival—and in the second coming, and the third—of money. Which beat his religion, he had to admit. There was nothing quite as dismal as the holy hope of escape.

"Look alive, people. Other business."

A hand went up in the far corner of the room. "Have you picked a date for sales conference?"

"And the location," someone chimed in.

"We've got to let the reps know. They have to book flights," someone else persisted. "We're talking about hundreds of flights to New York."

Dawn quieted them all with a thumb aimed at Oscar. "Place and date. You bet. Tell them, Oscar."

"Sure. Um." He looked down at his clipboard in despair.

"Oscar," she barked. "Hel-*lo*, Oscar."

"Tell me we have a date," Marion hissed in his ear. "There are five hundred people waiting to hear the date."

Which is how it came to him. "March sixteenth," he said.

"That's early. March is early."

"Where did he say?"

"Where's that, Oscar."

"Did you say the place?"

He looked up from his clipboard and around the room. "Think big," he said with a tentative smile.

The Food

SHE WALKED LIKE A STARLET in a black-and-white film across the dark plane of tinted glass as he watched from inside the restaurant. She entered and regained her color, approaching his booth past the hostess and long walls of wine. She was wearing a snug green dress and enough lipstick to sharpen the dazzle of her face. He stood up and cracked his knee on the table. Sat back down, spilling the breadsticks.

Lauren slid into her seat. Between the golden walls

and orange columns, diners cowered beneath the classical music and the establishment's reputation as if eating and conversing in a light rain. "So this is what you editors do all day," she said. "I had a feeling."

"You bet. Lunch after lunch after lunch." He scrambled to clean up the straws of bread and poke them back into their jar. "It's kind of an all-you-can-eat profession."

"Ha. So's mine."

"But I'm actually not an editor. I'm an assistant."

"Well, you're certainly assisting me. I can't believe you're taking me to lunch at Le Pouvoir." She smiled at the woman in the cape and cat-eye sunglasses who floated past their table toward the powder room. "I've always wanted to eat here. You're sure you can do this?"

"Of course. I'm in publishing. You're a writer. This is a business expense." He sat back. "How's your book going, anyway?"

"It's not. I haven't started. I'd like to, though." She hesitated. "Can I still eat the lunch?"

"I'll have to talk to the finance department."

"I'm dying to write a book. I'm just way too disorganized."

"Sounds like you need an editor."

"What I need," she said, "is an assistant."

"You got it."

"Ha." She carefully selected the tallest breadstick. "Tell me this, though, Oscar. Aren't most assistants about twenty-two years old?"

"They are. Yes."

"So how did—"

"And then they're twenty-five, and thinking of leaving for a job at a magazine until they realize that it would be no better, only with tighter deadlines and a flimsier product."

"That's probably true."

"And suddenly they're twenty-seven, and thinking they've been there way too long, which leads to the conviction that their experience has made them invaluable, and that it would take years to become that invaluable at any other job."

"I can see that."

"And a second later they turn thirty, and they realize that this has become their life. That every career has its cruelties, and every employee in the world has his gripes, and that these are mine. I own them. And there's no point restlessly exchanging them for others I know less well."

"So you stay."

"I stay, if you can believe it"—he almost laughed—"because I have nothing better to do."

They were silent with that until a waiter arrived and departed to fetch their bottle of champagne.

"Well, I know where you're coming from," she said.

"You know New Jersey?"

"No, I mean career-wise. I mean about being stuck."

"Oh."

"I feel like I'm watching the best years of my life go by. No, worse than that: of other people's lives. It's like I'm trapped behind the scenes."

"That's it."

"And they're not even my scenes."

"Yup. Same."

"At least you get to wear pretty ties."

He looked down.

"Those are lilies of the valley," she said. "On your tie."

"What, the flowers?"

"I love lilies of the valley."

"Huh. I would have thought you liked—"

"—roses. I know. LaRoses." She smiled kindly. "Men are so literal."

"We're not literal. We just don't know anything," he said. "In fact, I know less and less about anything the more I learn about weddings. I've lost more brain cells to the nitpicking lunacy of— Did you know, for example, that the cocktail shrimp for the raw bar are classified according to number per pound?"

"I did."

"As in 16-20s? And 21-25s?"

"I know."

He took a breadstick and pointed it at her before chomping off the end. "So what's a U-15."

"That's a hefty shrimp. Under fifteen to a pound."

"I'm doing food now."

"Poor you." Her dress moved greenly over her figure as she adjusted the napkin on her lap. "But you know what, Oscar? And I hate to say it. You brought this on yourself. All men do. You spend your lives completely ignoring the chance, let alone the particulars, of getting married. You grow up trying *not* to learn anything in advance, *not* asking or talking or even thinking about it on your own, so that when the time comes you have to be put through this fast-forward crash course on the whole thing. Which you fail."

"You're telling me little girls are taken aside and taught shrimp fractions?"

"No, but we will notice and remember a dress style. Plan our hairstyle. See, girls grow up dreaming of Prince Charming and wedding bells. Boys grow up with nightmares about balls and chains."

"I take it you have your wedding all planned."

"No way."

"I thought you just—"

"Not me," she said. "No."

A lordly gent in a velvet blazer arrived to install, beside their table, an ice-filled silver cannister on stilts. He showed the champagne, unplugged it with a muffled blast, and was gone before their flutes had stopped fizzing.

"Wowee."

"You must get taken out all the time," he said.

"Like this? Never."

"Don't you get comped at fancy restaurants? Wined and dined at places that want to be mentioned in the magazine?"

"Not once," she said. "I usually don't let people know who I am."

She smiled sadly at the truth of it, then up at Oscar. He looked huge, *felt* huge: a groom, at long last, who couldn't be whittled into ten paragraphs and sent off. She was used to sitting down and sizing things up, couple after couple for the magazine, date after pitiful date of her own. But there was no sizing up Oscar. The champagne cheered in her throat.

"So how do you keep them all straight?" he asked her. "All those weddings. They've got to blur together after a while."

"No, they're all different. Something always happens to distinguish the occasion. They're sort of labeled, in my memory, like Broadway plays. *The Vomiting Cousin. Dance of a Thousand Lawyers.*"

"I was at this wedding last February—a guy named Ken, from college—where the chuppah fell onto the ketubah and the cantor started to wail."

"The cantor's supposed to wail," she said. "I went to one in Connecticut where instead of the wedding march, the bride played a tape she'd secretly recorded the night before the ceremony. Of the groom. With her maid of honor."

"No."

"It's true. She walked all the way up to the altar, handed off her bouquet, and punched him out."

"I didn't read that column."

"I couldn't write it. I was clapping too hard to take notes."

As his gaze traveled the restaurant, she looked over her suede menu at the solidness of his shoulders and recalled the fit of his chin. She thought of the Amish couple from Pennsylvania (June issue, farm wedding) who were barred from physical contact for the first six months of their relationship. The pair from San Francisco (April issue, jazz club) who spent their first date having sex in a trolley car. Then she thought of his wedding. Her eyes dropped obediently back to her menu.

Oscar's, meanwhile, were riveted across the room on Gordon Fox. There was no mistaking that dwarfish figure, the half-bald head that somehow emphasized his hairiness elsewhere. He kept looking over at Dawn's table, empty in the far corner. He must have checked with the maître d' that she wouldn't be there. Gordy snaked his arms beneath the tablecloth. His dining companion, a young woman in what looked like a cheerleader's outfit, jerked backward with a horsey guffaw. Then she scooted forward. He lunged again. *Oh, Gordy,* she mouthed. A waiter stepped in, perhaps on purpose, to block Oscar's view.

"So tell me," Lauren was saying, "about the fiancée."

He felt sick. "The, um, fiancée. Well, if you want to know the truth" — but he stopped himself short. He couldn't lie to Lauren; still, he couldn't tell her the truth. "The truth is that she's hard to describe."

"Aha."

"She's, I don't know." He struggled to come up with a complimentary adjective for Dawn. "Strong-willed."

"That's probably good."

"Hardworking," he improvised.

"Is she tall?"

"Short."

"How funny."

"No, not particularly funny either."

She frowned. "Oh."

Oscar looked back at Gordy. "Then again, the groom's disgusting. So, you know. Fair's fair."

"You are not. Why would you —"

"The thing is," he said, "I'm not positive that this is going to work out."

"What, the marriage?"

"The wedding. It may not happen."

Dawn didn't deserve a life of Gordy Fox, he thought. If anyone did, she did; but she didn't. And if anyone could assist her to avoid it, it was Oscar. Dawn had fallen for this baboon out of some kind of midlife myopia, or else a corporate pragmatism; he could only hope for the latter. In either case she was being taken, and it was Oscar's responsibility to take her back. Bosses and assistants need each other, own each other. They come to each other's defense as automatically as they come to work.

"That's horrible. I'm so sorry." Lauren's lips, accordingly, made the shape of sorrow. But her eyes were alight, something kindling within them. "Is it her? Or you. Or do you not want to talk about it."

"It's him."

"Ah. There's a him. Say no more. That's the worst."

The waiter approached to discuss the selection of cursive entrées. It was hard not to tighten up in that place, to pay heed to proper diction when responding to the august pronouncements of its personnel. The soul of an English nobleman crept into Oscar's voice as he posited a question concerning the filet mignon.

"Po-*tah*-to?" she teased him when the waiter had left.

"What?"

"You said po-*tah*-to."

"I seized up. And I wouldn't talk: you said yours in French."

"I did not."

"Did too."

"I said *haricots verts*. Those are green beans."

"In France."

"*Touché.*"

"Cut it out," he said.

"Don't you speak any other languages?"

"Street slang. Pig Latin. I ride the subways every day, so I know the Spanish for *hemorrhoid*."

"We've got to get you out of this city, Oscar."

"Amen," he said.

He could hardly remember his mother. The flashes he had of her (extracting a splinter from his thumb, impersonating the Lilliputians as she read him

Gulliver's Travels) were difficult to distinguish from the two-dimensional snapshots that his father kept in New Jersey: a portrait on every wall, a stash of photos in every drawer. It was hard to retrieve a fork without seeing her in a straw hat on her thirty-fifth birthday, to rummage for a screwdriver without spotting her on a horse. He had encouraged his dad to get out of the house, to take up golfing or bowling, to try bridge. He ought to make an effort to meet people; but apparently he couldn't, just as his son couldn't persuade him. The man's loneliness pulsed in Oscar like an inheritable trait. He felt it in the empty length of his arms, saw it in the blankness of his expression when at night the windows of his apartment turned to mirrors and showed—inches away, looking out—only one. That was the part he didn't tell Lauren. That and the growing sense that such hollowness could be filled.

She had a clear memory of her father the morning he left for the hairdresser, stuffing undershirts into the paisley suitcase that she could have sworn was hers. It was by chance, due to flu, that his youngest daughter was at home to witness his preplanned departure with her brother and sister at school and their mother shopping for eggs. Knock-kneed and runny-nosed, Lauren had trailed him from room to room, suggesting shaving cream and pulling out boxer shorts in order to hurry him out. With the rickety slam of that screen door came the knowledge that men leave, a fact she never bothered to include in her monthly celebrations

of their arrival. She wrote love stories, she guessed—
and this she didn't tell Oscar—to fight off the conviction that they didn't exist. Writing itself was less of a
career choice than her admission of outsider status: of
her tendency toward the corners of parties and a fond-
ness for watching them from there. It might have to
do, she said, with being from far away.

"Where's far away?"

She swirled the remaining champagne in her glass.
"Idaho."

"The Gem State," he said.

"That's right."

"Forty-third to enter the union."

She coughed. "Are you into geography or something?"

"I edited a book on U.S. history. Learned my cap-
itals for the first time."

"You remember all that from a round of editing?"

"Well, I had to rewrite it," he said. "Write it, really."

"Idaho's wonderful."

"I know. Its domestic exportation of po-*tah*-toes
alone—"

"I'm not talking about potatoes, Oscar. It's beautiful there."

"I believe you," he said.

"The farmlands go on forever. The mountains loom
over you like—well, like *real* skyscrapers. Not like
these square-topped, building-block imitations."

"I'm sure."

"The Craters of the Moon. The River of No

Return. The Crystal Falls Cave. Did you know that Hell's Canyon is the deepest gorge on the continent?"

"I didn't," he said.

"Ha."

"I'd like to go sometime."

She put down her glass. "To *Idaho*? Why?"

"Isn't it obvious? The Crystal Craters! Hell's Bells River!"

"Hell's Canyon." She laughed. "Seriously, Oscar."

"I don't know why. Just to go. I haven't really gone anywhere."

"Well, I go everywhere. All the time. And I can tell you, it's overrated. I'd rather stay in one place."

"Not in my place, you wouldn't."

Two covered dishes were set before them, their gold domes yanked off with a double poof of steam. After clinking forks, they carefully inserted utensils into the sculptures on their plates. Her shish kebabs were served vertically. His steak was a perfect pentagon. And soon their conversation turned, as they had, to food.

There are those in life who see what they want and simply march up and take it. For them, think buffet. Others expect to be handed things on silver platters; in which case, seated meal. But whisked and folded into these decisions are further decisions to be made. Buffet can be a long display or separate stations. Sit-down can be French service, Russian style, or grabbed with good old American gusto from the family portion at the center of the table. Hors d'oeuvres may be passed or plated.

Colors of entrées ought not to clash. Japanese is particularly labor-intensive, Tex-Mex quick to turn heavy, lamb a gamble to reheat. Take stock of allergies and religions, of vegetarians and octogenarians, of numbers of babies and quantities of booze. Count 5 glasses per wine or champagne bottle, 25 in a jug of liquor, 260 to a keg — and you have yourself a steaming feast of calculations, a fresh spread of headache. Food for thought.

His binder barely fit on the table between all their champagne and water glasses and oversized plates. "You're going to be fearsome at this," he told her, closing the section marked Food.

"I will not."

"I mean when you plan your wedding."

"I'm not planning my wedding."

"But when you *do*." He smiled. "You're the queen of the realm. Given all your experience —"

"Given all my experience," she said, "count me out."

"You're not getting married?"

"Oh, I'm getting married. I'm just not planning it."

"Huh."

"You want to know *my* fantasy wedding, Oscar? I'll tell you my fantasy wedding." Her arms dropped onto the binder, her body curving toward his. "What I want is to walk into some place for the very first time, just before the ceremony, and get married. I don't care what it looks like or how many people show up. I don't want to think about the ring or fret over the stupid dress. I'd rather not know what was handpicked for the centerpieces or how many spices are in the mignonette sauce. Decent women across the country are dying slow deaths in the process of arranging the best day of their lives. Me, I just want to walk in."

"But you do," he said. "Every month."

"Not into *my* wedding. Not as the bride." She watched a businessman in a bow tie making orchestral air-swoops for his check. "All the people in place. All the touches . . . touched up. I'll arrive on time, kiss my mom, meet the guy, slip on the ring, and be married. Few minutes tops."

"You don't even want to know the groom?"

"Not too well. Maybe a little. I guess I could meet him somewhere first."

"An arranged marriage," he said. "How . . . modern."

"That's me."

What was it about weddings, Oscar wondered, that divorced their owners from all pleasure and sanity? What else drove competent women so quickly insane, drove the hardiest men underground, and prompted such intelligent exceptions as Lauren and Dawn to refuse the least involvement? A person planning a wedding sooner or later went berserk. Yet he was in no danger. He wasn't planning his own wedding; he was merely plotting Dawn's. Across the restaurant Gordy was guiding his girlfriend out past the coat-check booth with a hand on her rear. Or rather plotting, he decided, against it.

Lauren smiled at the waiter and accepted the dessert menu that he presented with enough saccharine fanfare to be a dessert itself.

She looked up and down the list. "Have you thought about cake?"

"I'm actually thinking about that plank-seared tart."

"I mean for your wedding."

"Oh," he said. "Not really. Not yet."

She thought for a moment. "What time do you have to be back at the office?"

"No rush. My boss is at her acupuncturist until three-thirty. Why?"

She waved over their waiter. He bent forward, hands behind his back, as she spoke to him in a low voice. When he started to list the dessert specials she motioned him closer, whispering now. Abruptly he left the table.

"What happened?" he asked her. "What did you say?"

"I accidentally let slip who I was. May have mentioned the magazine."

"You pulled rank."

She grinned. "I've never done this before."

"All hail the queen."

At that she stood and pushed in her chair.

"Where are you going?"

She curled a regal finger to summon him along. "Let us eat cake."

"It began with the ancient Romans."

The back room of the restaurant was a private chamber of oak walls, dimmed lamps, and a dark leather divan. The pastry chef had brought them dessert wines to sip as they sat and awaited his return.

"They used to burn barley cakes over a flame to consecrate the marriage," Lauren said. "Later they were crumbled over the bride's head as a fertility ritual."

"I could ask the chef about a barley cake," Oscar considered. "But if I know the bride—and I do—she's not going to take kindly to having dessert dumped on her head."

"I'd skip it. I tried barley at a Camelot wedding last month."

"As in the Kennedys?"

"As in King Arthur," she said. "Wild boar on the grill. Mugs of mead at the bar. The poor priest had to wear chain mail."

"You're joking."

"It wasn't all bad. I got to pull Excalibur out of the ice sculpture."

The pastry chef reappeared wheeling a cart and wearing a tall white hat, having thrown aside his hairnet when their waiter had found him at the back of the steamy kitchen and chased him excitedly out. Oscar and Lauren rose to be guided, in a soggy Parisian accent, through the slices that pointed in various directions, like ivory sundials, on all three levels of the cart.

"What you can't see here," she told him, "is the architecture."

"*L'architecture*," the chef agreed, nodding his hat.

"These cakes would all be tiered. Tiers can be either *separated*—elevated off each other, in other words, by something decorative—or *stacked*."

"Separated or stacked," Oscar repeated.

"*C'est quoi, ça?*" she asked the chef.

"*C'est un gâteau de genoise et dacquoise.*"

"No secrets, you two."

"*Et ça? C'est pas ganache.*"

"*Mais oui, madame, c'est ganache.*"

"*Eh bien,*" she said. "*Je le savais.*"

"That'll do."

She turned toward him. "Always pretend you know more than you do," she whispered. "That's rule number one."

He stepped forward. "*Frère Jacques?*" He pointed at a slice curly with white chocolate shavings. "*Frère Jacques? Dormez-vous?*"

"Oscar."

But the man was beaming. "*Bien fait. Frère Jacques. La chanson.*"

"What? He agreed."

"They always agree," she said. "That's rule number two."

"Can we taste? Taste?" he asked.

"*Oui.* You can *taste-uh.*"

Oscar smiled as if amazed. Lauren shook her head and moved beside him.

Buttercream won bilateral acclaim. Split vote on Swiss meringue with mocha filling. Carrot cake encrusted with walnuts and silver shot dragées initiated a debate over incorporating vegetables into dessert that had to be translated for the chef, who agreed with both sides. In Bermuda, Lauren said as they shared the cheesecake with apricot filling (two thumbs down), the cake is topped by a tiny sapling to symbolize new life. In Denmark they eat eighteen layers of almond meringue. According to the tradition of the Lorraine Valley, the bride and groom have to kiss over a dish piled high with waffles. Oscar barely managed to get down the basket-woven spice cake before expressing his preference for waffles.

"You have to try the spun sugar." She pointed to the spindly cloud that surrounded a wedge of yellow and white.

"That's sugar? It looks like insulation."

"Never mind, then. Have a *croquembouche*." On a plate beside a pink rose was perched a single puff pastry coated with caramel.

"I'm stuffed."

"Get out of here. Look at you. I'd bet you can eat forever."

"Fine. Throw it."

"No."

"Pass," he said. "Toss it here. You think I can't catch? Varsity center on the high school basketball team."

"Varsity pitcher on the high school softball team," she replied, patting herself above the neckline of her dress.

"Then chuck it in here, Lauren. Bear down."

She glanced at the chef, who was pensively wiping his chin. The man looked down at the pastry—and then scooped it up himself and tossed it with a snigger across the room. Stretching high, Oscar stabbed it out of the air.

"*Hup-la!*"

"Nice save," she agreed.

"*Vous devriez vous préparer pour l'autre, les amants!*" The man was pretending to mash something in front of his face. He looked to Lauren. "*Préparez-vous en avance.*"

"Is he telling me to shut up?" Oscar asked. "He's right. You're right. I'm sorry." He was eating the *croquembouche* like an apple. "Tell him this is fantastic."

"Here." She clapped. "Let me taste."

"Oh, I don't think so."

"Come on. Fastball." She hiked up her dress and set her feet.

"It'll explode on the wall."

"I can catch, Oscar."

"*Allez!*" coached the chef.

"If you say so. Here goes."

He lofted the pastry. She clapped while it was in the air, showing off, before catching it cleanly between the heels of her hands. "Ha!"

"*Ouai—comme ça, mais plus près!*" He was back to

pantomiming the crushing of something in someone's face. *"Pah! Comme les mariés! Pah! Allez!"*

Oscar's follow-through and shallow toss had brought him and Lauren nearly face-to-face. They watched each other smile with their mouths full.

"Isn't it great?" he said.

"It's great."

"Alors, maintenant sur le visage," the chef encouraged.

"What's he saying?"

"Nothing. He thinks we're— No, nothing."

"Allez! Vite!"

The man lost patience and, with a hand on each of their backs, shoved them together. And before she could lift the rest of the *croquembouche* or he could politely halt their collision they had crashed, stooping downward and tiptoing upward, into a kiss.

The Flowers

I T IS WITH GLEE, and with terror, that one discovers it
can be done: that the day can be assembled out of
phone calls and faxes of confirmation, love's crowning
moment thoroughly researched and paid for in advance.
That weddings are planned, in a word. That more
fervent attention to detail—engraved versus thermographed, rose petals over rice—can make the one-of-a-
kind occasion ever so slightly more so. In an earthly
existence marked by unpredictable births and unfore-

seeable deaths, it's the one such momentous event that can be calibrated to the minute, to the dollar, to the endless aggravation of the person in charge. Like lightning before thunder, this bright realization unleashes a storm of blueprints and price lists, a rising tide of tasks that threatens to drown the planner in fathomable grief.

He hadn't been quite himself in the office. He was paler, more harried, his customary efficiency beginning to break down. He brewed a pot of clear coffee without having added the grounds. He mismarked a FedEx package that arrived the next morning back on his desk. Four and a half months away, and already the wedding was leaking into his routine and eroding his system of systems. But fall was the high season in book publishing, a time when blockbusters were catapulted at customers and middle-aged editors jogged in the halls, and his mishaps seemed to go unnoticed. So, too, did his top-secret progress. He had the date, had the place. He was missing a minister but had settled the food.

"Hello, Dawn Books."

"Fox Agency," said a female voice in greeting. "Hold for Gordon Fox."

There was Muzak on hold. There were days, entire years of his life, spent yessing and noing on the phone, picking up and hanging up and accomplishing nothing at all. He would have to do more than that if he wanted to save Dawn from Gordy. His candid attempts to enlighten his boss had been met, mid-sentence, with the fury of a woman who had no time for talk. Action would be required.

He finished filing the latest reviews and logging the morning's manuscript submissions with the receiver vised between his jaw and shoulder. He refilled his basket of candy corns from the soap-smelling bag in his bottom drawer. It was almost Halloween. It was only eleven o'clock. He lifted the current edition of the magazine before his face, opened to "Aisle of White." This month featured a photo of what looked like a telescope. A wedding in Arizona. A voice in his ear.

"Fox Agency," said a man this time. "Holding for?"

"Gordon. But I didn't actually call—"

"Name?"

"My name? Oscar. I'm just Daw—"

"Hold."

He looked back to the magazine. He read the first paragraph again. Her other line rang, and he thought of clicking off to get it. Two more rings, one more ring, and he'd get it.

"Mr. Fox is unavailable. Is there something a member of his staff could help you with?"

"Nothing, no. He called *me.*"

"So you're returning."

"I'm not doing anything."

"Well, I'm afraid that—"

The man was blipped away.

"Oscar. Gordy."

"Oh, hey, Gordy. There was a little mix-up there."

"Don't sweat it, pal. We're man-to-man here. I'm not gonna tell your boss you fucked up on the phone."

"I didn't fu— Anyway. Dawn's in an advertising meeting until noon."

"So how's it hanging."

"Fine. You?"

"Outstanding," he said. "You taking care of my boy?"

Oscar scoured his desk, checked his bulletin board, peered at his computer screen for a name. His boy. The name of his boy. "Kirk Connolly," he guessed.

"Who else? That's my main man. And now he's *your* main man. He's going to call you later to touch base. Get his ass kissed. Because he's the man. Am I right? You saw *Final Explosion*."

"Some of it, sure. On video."

"*Lethal Invasion*."

"I meant to, yes."

"*Primal Aggression*."

"In fact, I'm thinking of renting a triple feature with—"

"Gotta put you on hold, kid."

He put aside the magazine. He refilled his stapler to the watery beat of a samba.

"Better keep my man happy," Gordy said upon his return.

"Of course." It seemed appropriate, at this juncture, to launch into the standard line: "We're all very proud to be publ—"

"'Cause if you don't, we're outta here. I pull my author and I put him somewhere else. And I go too. Never heard from again. *Fffft:* gone. Like one of those—what do you call those things in the desert.

You think they're right there, but then—you know those things. What I'm saying is this. You keep us happy, pal, and we won't take off."

"And otherwise you will," Oscar said. He was thinking out loud.

"Got that right. I'll be gone. And I don't think anyone wants that."

"No."

"Don't think your boss wants that."

"She doesn't."

"Think she kinda likes having me around."

"You can rest assur—"

"So what are you doing with yourself, Big O?" There was the creak of a chair. "Going out. Getting laid."

"Not really, no."

"C'mon. You're a dog. Surrounded by girls in that office. Rubbing up against what's-her-tits. Marion. Can't tell me you're not a dog."

The tin-can echo of Gordy's speakerphone made this turn in the conversation particularly uncomfortable. "Okay. I'm a dog."

"Yeah, you're a dog just like me. Although I've had to keep a leash on myself lately." With a clatter he picked up the phone to speak privately. "Due to circumstances of which you're aware of."

"Actually, I meant to ask you about that. Man to man. Didn't I see you at lunch, a couple weeks ago, with a young—"

"All right, big dog." He laughed a phlegmy laugh. "So how's it coming. The project."

Oscar sighed. "Coming along, I guess. I found a caterer who—"

"Marcy!"

"Sorry?"

"Marcy, get that dildo to wait another minute, will you? Get him some coffee. Spill water on him. Do something. I'll be out in one minute. O? Gotta boogie."

"I'll have her call." He pulled the magazine in front of him.

"Outstanding. Take care of my boy, now."

"You got it."

"And my girl," he said.

"Will do. Goodb—"

"Get her some flowers or something."

"Flowers? From you?"

"You bet. Marcy will call you back with my card number. Something fancy. Costly. I want to kick her ass with these things."

"With flowers."

"There you go. I'll leave the color and kind and all that crap in your hands. Although I'm thinking white."

"I don't blame y—"

"Gotta run, fella."

"Right."

"Kiss his ass for me."

"Kirk Connolly's? Sure."

"And pinch Marion's ass for me."

"Um—"

"And get some ass for yourself. What the hell are you doing over there? Marcy!" He smashed off the line.

High on a hill in Tucson, Arizona, stands an observatory often visited on local school field trips and revered by astrophysicists across the nation. Steward Observatory is home to some of the world's most advanced aerospace technology, including the Heinrich Hertz Submillimeter Telescope, the most accurate radio telescope ever built. The site has also been instrumental in such feats as the successful installation of the Near Infrared Camera and Multi Object Spectrograph aboard the Hubble Space Telescope in 1997. And even more impressive than that, it brought together Travis and Jen.

"They were two peas in a pod—or two asteroids in a belt," remembers Matthew Schmunk, Ph.D., who introduced the couple in 1995 after all three happened to attend a joint colloquium on the evolution of circumstellar disks. Although Professor Schmunk could hardly have imagined that he would serve as best man at their wedding four years later, he did have an inkling of the pair's instantaneous bond. "Two planets in a system," he amends. "I say planets because planets possess gravity, much like Jen and Travis. These two have pull for each other, magnetic attraction, and they had it the moment they met. And that's extremely rare in this universe. Or any universe, for that matter. Or any matter."

Dark matter, in fact, is what brought both Travis Brewster, Ph.D., and Jennifer Fidkin, Ph.D., to Tucson that weekend: specifically, his long-term study of baryon in the galaxy's dark matter halo and her related paper on the critical density for cosmological flatness. But there was nothing dark about the Saturday afternoon that the couple, both 32, recited vows culminating in Neil Armstrong's famous one-small-step-for-man line before fifty friends and colleagues in the observatory where they first met.

They were married in the Mirror Laboratory, a white-bricked room dominated by a 6.5-meter Magellan I primary mirror currently being polished before its insertion into a telescope. The ceremony was conducted by a nondenominational minister in a pointy Merlin hat stenciled with suns and moons. While the bride was dressed as a shooting star, complete with glitter in her hair and a tinfoil train on her dress, and the groom could barely be heard through his sealed cosmonaut's helmet, it was the guests who stole the show, having been asked to come as their favorite astronomical body. Three friends arrived as Orion's belt, two Saturns chatted over their rings by the bar, and Jennifer's mother's ET costume boasted a glowing finger. The party

dined on green cheese and Milky Way bars
as the University of Arizona band played
the theme songs of *Star Wars, Star Trek,*
and *A Star Is Born.*

"Before Jen, Travis wasn't a particularly fun-loving guy," admits his younger
brother Stan, 28. "He only cared about
all his charts and calculations. But now
he's in love with a person, too, and
that's loosened him up a lot. I had never
seen him dance."

Dance Travis did as the party got row-
dier, the band got louder, and inter-
galactic costumes were discarded to
reveal the tank tops and miniskirts of a
populace better known for their figures
on molecular cloud cores. Toward the end
of the event, the groom had to be talked
down from his solo disco romp atop the
surface of the parabolic mirror, having
clearly made, over the course of the
evening, a giant leap for his kind.

Sooner or later, like a gift to the gardener, after months of
toil and whole seasons spent making deposits and nur-
turing the seeds of a successful occasion, things bloom.

Bouquets are biedermeier and tussy mussy,
nosegay and posie, crescent and composite and cas-
cade. They are held at the waistline, elbows on hip-
bones; tossed over the head, wrist snapped for extra
height. Tied, wired, and stuffed into centerpieces, they
are bluebell and viburnum, freesia and hydrangea—
and annoying if not trimmed below the eye level of

seated guests. They are roses in fishbowls, tulips in breakaways, still lives of calla lilies with kumquats on the buffet. The quiet art of Ikebana. The grotesquery of a topiary. Beware the thorns of presentation; for yellow flowers are given by Iranians to their enemies, and the Chinese use white blossoms to mourn. Striped carnations meant refusal to the early Victorians. "Floral designer" means a bigger bill from the florist. Watch for loose leaves in water, which may start to reek. Use caution when scattering fresh petals, as they can upend the bride. Afterward you can air-dry the bouquet and boutonniere, freeze-dry the head table display, stir-fry a blossom into your first marital meal. Or else pluck and collect them into a potpourri: a wafting reminder of the color and calm of flowers, as well as the stink of having to entwine them into an event.

Oscar studied the notes on flowers that Lauren had dictated the day before. After trying out a pronunciation of *deciduous* and practicing his spelling of *cyclamineus*, he reached over the binder to call back the floral designer for the third time that day.

"I'm just not sure we need—"

"Pavé arrangements on the tables, greenery on the bar, magnolia arches by the dance floor, cabbage roses throughout."

He wrote down her recommendation. "It just sounds like a lot of—"

"Plenty of flowers means color, it means fragrance, it makes for ambiance." She was one of those wedding professionals—by now he'd met many—who spoke only in lists. Who listened not at all. "The look will be luxurious, you'll be pleased, she'll be thrilled." She was punching the order into her computer. "But it's up to you," she added. "It's your day."

He had been told that repeatedly. "Is it, though?"

"Is it what."

"It's up to me? Honestly? It's my day?"

"Yours and the bride's. Of course it is."

"And what if I want no flowers at all?"

Marion appeared outside her office and started up the hallway.

He turned toward the wall. "What if I decided to order, say, *zero* flowers from you?" he asked quietly.

"Naturally," the woman answered, "I would have to argue against that."

Marion stopped by the water fountain to pick at her stocking, still out of earshot.

"And what if I were to request only poison sumac. Piled on the tables. Draped across the bandstand."

"I really don't have time to —"

"Or just one flower. A single dandelion. Smack in the center of the room in a paper cup."

She could no longer hold back. "I would say that was silly."

"So you'd say no."

Marion stood before him. He formed the words *Do you need something?* She pointed, with a broad smile, to the magazine at the corner of his desk.

"Naturally I would say no. I have served as floral designer at more than a hundred weddings, over thirty bar mitzvahs, a dozen parades, two pageants, a christen —"

"So it's actually *not* my day," he said. "And it's not her day. It's *your* day."

"It is not," said the woman, "*my* day."

"It is! It's your day!" He was yelling now. "Your day to shine, to have everything go according to *your* plan, with *your* flowers. You don't need my opinion at all. You just need a day. And now you have it. Your very own day. Congratulations. All the best to you, on your very special day."

She had hung up. Marion was staring. He replaced the receiver.

"What, Marion?"

She took a candy corn from the basket. She bit off the yellow segment and then the orange and finally popped the tiny white pill onto her tongue. "Who was that?"

"That was the agent on, um, *The Wonder of Wildflowers.*"

"She's a loon."

"You're telling me."

"Was it about sales conference?"

"It was, yes, about sales conference. She wants to make it her own special day. And I said no. As you heard."

Marion scooped and juggled a few more candy corns in her hand, eyeing him. She didn't buy it.

"I said absolutely not," he went on. "I told her we have other big-name authors to launch at the conference. Tommy Gunn. Cherry Margaret. Kirk Connolly, for God's sake. We're not going to treat her gardener with kid gloves." He took a tissue from his top drawer and wiped off his computer screen. He busied himself with the fastidious untangling of his phone cord. He would have to call back the floral designer and apologize. He had to check on the chairs—there was the question of white versus wood—and to make preliminary inquiries about registering for gifts. But he had to wait for Marion to leave.

"There's a new girl in design," she said.

"So I hear. Deborah. Have you met her?"

"Not your type."

"I wasn't asking if she was my type. I just wanted to know—"

"What *I* want to know," she said, coming to the point, "is when you got to be such a faithful reader of 'Aisle of White.'"

"Me? I'm not." He shrugged. "I mean, every so often I—you know. Take a look."

"And take notes." She touched a fingernail to his open binder.

"Those aren't notes on— Yes. Those are notes," he said. "The column this month happens to feature two astronomers. And, as you'd know if you read the memo from contracts, we happen to have a book on space exploration coming out next year. See Marion, here in the editorial department, we employ various techniques of—"

"That's not it," she said. "You're up to something."

"I am not."

"Oscar." She put her wrists on her hips and moved her shoulders lasciviously, if woodenly. "I have ways," she breathed, "of making you talk."

Carl arrived to interrupt the show and place a misspelled book jacket on top of Oscar's In box. "Please inform Dawn, my dear boy, of that pesky *i*-before-*e* rule." He looked at Marion, who hadn't taken her eyes off Oscar. "Oh, what now." He folded his arms. Something crinkled in his hand and reminded him. "I nearly forgot," he said, pushing forward a few curly pieces of fax paper. "This came for you a few minutes ago."

Let fall onto the book jacket, the pages flattened to reveal the first draft of the January column. At the top was the clear signature of Lauren LaRose, as well as a line—legible by all three of them—wishing him luck on the flower front.

"Well, well," said Marion.

"If you two will excuse me, I have some filing to do for Dawn. Before she gets out of the ad meeting. If you'll excuse me."

"I know what this is about."

"No, you don't."

"You have something to do for Dawn, all right. But it's not filing."

"Marion."

"The world can be divided into two types of people," she declared. "Those who know, and those who have to hear it from me. So now hear this." She basked in the moment. Megaphoned her hands around her mouth. "Dawn and Gor—"

"I'm getting married."

Her hands fell. "What did you say?"

"I'm going to get married. You heard me. I'm engaged."

"You *are?*" Marion squawked. "To *who?*"

"To *whom*," Oscar replied, and was rewarded with a nod from Carl. "Just a woman I know. That's why I've been asking you two about weddings, and reading 'The Aisle of White.' I'm engaged. To be married."

"But who's the girl?"

"You don't know her, Marion. She's not from New York."

"I don't believe it."

"Well, I do," Carl offered. "I do indeed. This young man is a catch. He's a—what's the expression, now—*dish*. Good show."

"Thank you."

"Yeah. Whatever," said Marion. "Congratulations."

"Thanks. Now I really do have to make a few calls. I'm trying to plan this thing while Dawn's not around."

"Certainly."

"If you say so."

"And I'd really appreciate it if you guys could keep this a secret. Marion?"

"I heard you," she said. "So when's the wedding?"

"Four months."

"Four months? You'd better hustle."

"I'm hustling." His phone, Dawn's line, was ringing.

"Have you arranged the honeymoon?"

"Not yet. I should get this."

"Registered for gifts? Done your invitations?"

"Talk to you guys later," he said.

"Gotten a band?"

"Hello, Dawn Books?"

He watched the two of them walk back down the
hall together, looking back every few steps and whispering as if united in friendship by the shock of the
news.

Hello, Dawn Books. Hellodawnbooks. Helldabooks.
Hellwithbooks.

If people were meant to spend all day on the
phone, wouldn't we have higher shoulders and
shorter necks by nature? Wouldn't our rear ends
have evolved by now to something less bony and
shifting? And wouldn't those of us over six-foot-six
have conveniently, along with our ambitions, shrunk
to size?

"Hello, Dawn Books?"

There was the crackling preverbal quiet of someone important. "This," said the man, "is Kirk
Connolly."

"Oh, hello, Mr. Connolly. It's an honor. I'm
Dawn's assistant. How are you?"

"I was wondering," he intoned, "if I might have a
word with Dawn."

"I'm afraid she's not available. She's in a mee—
um." He shut his eyes. Bolstered his will. It was for
her own good. "She's at the track," he said.

"The horse track?"

"The dog track. I'm afraid. Can I take a message
for her?"

"She goes to the *dog track*?"

"Every day. I know." He was doubled over. Bent,
nonetheless, on sticking to the plan. "Old habits die
hard," he managed.

The author must have dropped the phone to his
chest. "My new publisher is at the track," he yelled
faintly to someone. "That's right. Gambling on dogs."

"Isn't the book business all about gambling on
dogs, though? Mr. Connolly?"

"I'm here."

"Overpriced investments. Thoroughbred per-
formers. Dark horse winners. It's all a day at the
track."

"I suppose so."

"Why don't we just say she's in a meeting?" he suggested. "Because that's essentially what it is. Let's call
it a business meeting. No different from any other
meeting at a publishing house these days."

The new girl from the design department, Deborah,
wandered in front of his desk and directly into Dawn's
office. He watched her incredulously as she threw down
a memo on Dawn's chair. Turning to leave, she upset the
thin porcelain vase at the edge of the desk and it cracked
in two, spilling its single white orchid.

"So then," Kirk Connolly said tiredly. "She's in a meeting."

"I'll have her call you." Oscar hung up the phone and rushed forward to save Deborah's life.

The floral designer was much nicer when he called her back to place the order. And no wonder. Lilies of the valley were normally available for a scant two weeks in May, and he needed them now. Such custom-coddled flowers would cost $600 per handheld bunch; he wanted a boxful. The woman typed at an ecstatic pace. They would be shipped to the magazine, the bride would be pleased with his choice, they would be just the effect he was after, he wouldn't regret the expense. To her list he added numbers: sixteen of them plus the expiration date. A few thousand dollars were unlikely to be noticed on the monthly statement of a monster agent. Nor would the charge for the second order — it could almost have been a shipping fee — of $19.99.

This had been possible, he thought as he sat back in his chair, all along. Things could be controlled not from the control room, but from the flimsy cubicle just outside it. He had been aware of this access, held these tinkling keys to power, but had always felt weighed down by them rather than set free. He thought of the assistants all over the city, huddled across the country, who held the lives of their superiors in the palms of their trembling hands, and he pitied their lack of initiative. *We have been given the credit card numbers*, he would proclaim to their legions over a loudspeaker, fax them all in capital letters, e-mail the lot of them in 72-point type. *Our memories contain all the nicknames, our files all the prescriptions, our Rolodexes all the information we need to take over our worlds.*

When Dawn returned from lambasting the advertising department, his feet were propped on his desk. He convulsed and took them down. "Jackasses," she announced as she clomped past. "I'm surrounded by jackasses." He gathered his clipboard and her messages and followed her in. She had thrown off her white blazer like a doctor entering the ER and was pushing around items on her desk. "Hell are my messages?"

"Right here." He spread them in their mandatory arc as she sat.

"You order those apples?"

"I did." He went back to close the door. "Freshest available. No bruises. Your doorman will have them by five-thirty."

"Peeled? I said peeled, Oscar. I asked for them peeled. I'm not going to spend an hour peeling apples like a goddamn kitchen worker."

"The store manager promised to peel them himself." He attempted a smile. "Making dinner for you-know-who?"

"Don't ask me questions, Oscar."

"Right. Sorry."

"Dessert," she grumbled.

He watched her as she pecked at her keyboard. Dawn was making a man dessert. This was no conniving megamerger: it was love, plain and simple, overwhelming the savage instincts and brute manners of even her. This was more serious than he thought. Frantically he decided to give the truth one more try. "Are you two still, I don't know, seeing other people? Because oddly enough, I saw —"

"If you ask me one more question," she said, "you will not. See other people. Ever again."

He sat down.

"Is Tommy Gunn on board for sales conference?"

"He is," Oscar said, perusing his clipboard. "Confirmed. He's a definite."

"That's not good enough."

"He'll be there."

"And you believe that. Have you tried to talk to that guy? Have you heard him speak? You go see that brain-dead bastard yourself and get me a guarantee that he'll be there. Put him in a cage and wheel him to the conference if you have to."

"Will do." He made note of the assignment. "Deborah from design stopped by."

"Fuck her."

"And Carl found a typo on the cover of *Moonlight in Missouri.*"

"Fucking tight-ass. *Fuck.*" She grabbed a message slip. "Kirk Connolly called?"

"He did. Around two-fifteen."

"It says two-nineteen here. Which is it?"

"Two-nineteen. Whatever I wrote."

"*Whatever I wrote,* he says. Why didn't you come get me?"

"You were in with the ad department. You said no calls."

"Dammit, Oscar. What did you tell him?"

"I told him you were in a meeting."

"Listen to me," she said. "Kirk Connolly is *big.* Kirk Connolly is *bigger* than big. Do you know what big is?"

"Yes."

"So tell me. When you deal with a big author—and this is a big, *big* author—what do you do?"

"Treat them big."

"Damn right."

"I apologize," he said.

"Yes you do. You apologize to Kirk Connolly when you get him on the phone for me. Immediately. And you apologize again when you give him my handwritten note along with two tickets to—what. *What,* Oscar. Something big. Something safe. Clean. The guy's a right-wing wacko."

"How about *Clog!*"

"The goddamn dance show?"

"It's Norwegian," he assured her. "Hottest thing on Broadway. Good clean fun. Cast of hundreds. Loud as anything. It's practically impossible to get tickets."

"Like hell it is. You call Howie and tell him they're for me."

"Harry. No problem."

"And then you deliver them to Duane Street or wherever he lives."

"Jane Street. Sure."

"With my note," she said. "And write me a note."

He added, beneath the crossed-out "apples" and the underlined "Tommy Gunn," a "Kirk Connolly" and a *"Clog!"* "It may take a while. A couple months at least. This is the Norse God of Dance we're talking about. He was on the cover of *Time.* The show's booked sol—"

"Got two weeks," she said.

There was a tremulous knock on the door.

"No," she said simply. Not loudly.

The knocking stopped.

"Who the fuck is this, Oscar? An author?" She shook another slip at him. "Never heard of him. Why do I have this message? This is a *small* author, Oscar. Say it, Oscar. *Small.* And how do you treat small authors."

"You don't."

She mashed and threw the wad of paper. "So why do you bother me with these sma—"

Another pattering on the door.

"What?"

"Dawn?" It was Marion. "There's a delivery for you."

"Get it, Oscar. Go get it."

He was up and at the door, pulling it ajar. After an exchange of looks with Marion, he took the gargan-

tuan thing by its black wicker handles and transport-
ed it onto the pale table in the middle of the room.

"What is *that*? Get those— Shit, Oscar. Don't put
those on my— Who the hell?"

He backed to the door and closed it on Marion.
"They're from Gordy," he whispered.

"What." She stammered for a moment. "What are
they?"

They were carnations, although it was hard to tell.
They were dyed orange and black, fringed with yellow
ribbons and arranged in the enormous shape of a gap-
toothed jack-o'-lantern. Oscar covered his smile with
his clipboard. They were perfectly awful.

The Music

I<small>N EVERY PLAN</small> there are pitfalls, long moments of
terror when the best-laid intricacies unravel. Wires
are crossed, sites double-booked, reservations
blipped from a screen, and you panic. Ten, a hundred
and twenty, half a thousand revelers soon to crowd
into the event—without chairs. Proud and jowly rel-
atives flocking from all over the globe to waltz in
one's honor—without music. Have faith, nevertheless, that things tend to come together, the way hus-

bands and wives do. Half by accident. Against the odds.

He crossed Fifty-sixth Street in a mob of jay-walkers, tramping toward the cold end of a dark Friday like everyone else. A homeless woman sneered when he dodged toward her to hand over change. An oily liquid dripped from an unseen windowsill to splatter his shoulder bag. In New York City moods are as infectious as a winter flu, and the place had picked up on his misery and was giving him a dose of it back.

She wasn't returning his calls. For the last two weeks he had left messages for her at the main desk of the magazine, the only phone number he had. Although she'd mentioned a wedding in Texas, he knew that she had long since returned. She had made a decision: he could feel it in the weight of the quiet of the phone. If he had her home number, he could clear up the impasse. She was leaving him alone out of a phantom respect for his nonexistent fiancée, as a result of his deception: he had given her no choice. But he'd had no choice either. This was all Dawn's fault, he thought. Yet Dawn's faults inevitably, professionally, belonged to him. He would write Lauren a letter. He was more confident on paper; improved by his editing, safe from stuttering. He would take his chances and tell her the whole story. What could happen? Dawn might murder him for turning over her top secret; but she murdered him anyway, more or less, every day.

Until then he would have to endure his purgatory, keep his head and get things done despite the sour lack of Lauren. The dead fact of her silence was a grating pain in his throat, a sledgehammer to his chest. The thought of her setting out to meet someone else—striding determinedly into the gaunt battalion of men who surrounded him now, on Fifty-seventh Street—made him want to curl up beside the mayhem of Fifth Avenue and weep. Or else sprint through the traffic, tromping long-legged on the hoods and bumpers, until he found her. But he didn't have time. Men must work, you see. Nose to the metal. Pedal to the grindstone. Without Lauren's expertise, with three and a half months and counting, it was up to Oscar to book a band.

He crossed Fifty-eighth and turned left toward the spitting fountain and drooping flags of the Plaza Hotel. He wove through the doormen, took the front stairs three at a time, hurried around the dining room and back toward the lobby elevators on the Central Park side. From down the gilded hallway came the chortles and ringing glasses of the bar crowd. He pictured the scene as he waited to go up: wealthy men and merry women clearing up all their misunderstandings at tables for two. He had no right to join them, he thought. If he had been honest with Lauren from the start, he might be seated with her in the midst of that jovial candor instead of standing alone, sorely mistaken, grimacing like a child on his way to his music lesson.

Chris had suggested drinks at the Plaza to cheer Lauren up, and for a time the venerable Oak Bar appeared to have the desired effect. Over sixteen-dollar martinis they took wild guesses at the private lives of their neighbors. A Swiss-German stockbroker strolled by to chat up Lauren; Chris, in retaliation, made eyes at his wife. Two gentlemen from Oman sent them over a round of cognac, which they promptly gave to the busboys from Mexico, who downed them like shots. But gradually Lauren returned to her funk. The Texas wedding had been a wearying hoot—the groom lassoing the bride, guests corralled into line-dancing—and still, ten days later, she hadn't written the piece. She handed her lame attempts at an opening across the table.

"*It took Jason Cook two years to rope this dogie,*" Chris read, affecting the accent, "*an' little did he know he was in for the raaad of his laaaf.* That's terrible."

"That's my best one."

"*If the stars at night are big and bright deep in the heart of Texas, then so were the eyes of Bridget Doherty on a recent Saturday mor*— I can't even read this."

"Tell me about it. I'm screwed."

"What happened to your assistant?"

"I don't want to talk about that."

Chris handed back the pieces of paper. "Remind me not to ask you to edit my dissertation," she said. "*If Jesus Christ is the unseen guest at every table, then Chris Lucas has cooked him the meal of his life in this three-hundred-page treatise on lesbian priestho*—"

"Very funny." Lauren felt upward for the lily she'd pinned in her hair. The entire curly load of them had clung to life admirably while she was in Texas, perfuming her apartment in their clusters, in her cups and soda bottles, to her delight.

"Nice flower," said Chris.

"Thanks."

"Gotta love flowers. Flowers say so much."

"Chris."

"I'm just saying." She drank her drink. "He sent you those, didn't he?"

"I'm not talking about this. You said I didn't have to talk about it."

"All I'm saying is that when a woman is sent flowers, it's generally meant as a sign of affection. And should she be sent an entire freaking parade float of her favorite—"

"Cut it out."

"I am. I'm just saying."

Lauren looked toward the door. "He's engaged."

"I know he's engaged. And *you've* known he's engaged. To someone he obviously doesn't care for, and who obviously doesn't care for him."

"So? That's someone. He's engaged to someone."

"And therefore you're dropping the whole idea."

"Yes."

"Ignoring the possibility. Firing the assistant."

"Stop calling him the assistant," she said.

"Well, stop saying he's engaged. I really don't think that's the problem here. Your problem is something else."

"Really. So what's my problem."

Chris leaned forward and blew her hair out of her eyes. "You have a problem with men."

"Ha. Look who's talking."

"I don't have a problem with men. I just don't happen to love any of them," she said. "You love one of them."

Lauren looked again at the door, then down at her discarded papers. "Maybe my life's too full of other people's stupid love stories to start my own."

"Maybe you write other people's love stories in order to avoid starting your own."

"That's ridiculous."

"Isn't it?"

"No, I'm saying—"

"I thought you weren't talking about it."

"I'm not," she said. "We're not." She sulked into her glass.

"An' another lone cowgirl raaads off across the prairie. Sun settin'. Saddle squeakin'. Eyes searchin' the horizon for a maaan—"

"Chris."

"I'm done."

"Dawn Books!" shouted Tommy Gunn when his hotel security team introduced the sky-high young man at the door. "Aw-*ri-i-i-i-ight!* Bam! Dawn Books in the house! Hey Potty!" He turned toward the bathroom, skinny in his ripped black T-shirt. Around his neck was a junkyard of metal rings and skulls. "My publisher's here!"

"Shit, it's a party!" said Potty. It sounded as if there were several people in the bathroom.

"What time is it? What the hell *month* is it?"

"It's about seven o'clock," Oscar answered. "November. I called before. I don't know if you got the message. I think I talked to someone named Cruller."

Tommy Gunn scratched at the spikes of his hair. He looked at his wrist for a minute before appearing to register the absence of a watch. Up his bare arms were long blocks of tatoos that, having undoubtedly started as a few potent images of ghoulish fates and voluptuous prizes, had been overcrowded into a sort of humdrum wallpaper of the flesh. In one hand he held a mini-cassette recorder. "You here for the book? Because I don't got it," he said. "I'll be straight with you: that other guy's writing it. The *Rolling Stone* guy."

"I didn't come for the book. You have until sales conference to get that done. Or your ghostwriter does."

"Cool."

"You *will* be at sales conference," Oscar said. "In March."

"No doubt."

"Will you? You promise? It's pretty important."

Tommy stuck a finger in a nostril. "Scout's honor."

Oscar was standing, he suddenly noticed, on the crushed edge of what looked like a deep-dish pizza submerged in the rug. He stepped off and into the suite. There were two bedrooms, a sitting room, a dining room, a full-sized fridge. Sticking out from the open freezer compartment was the neck of an electric guitar. "I actually came by," he said, "to ask you about a wedding."

"No-o-o-o-o. No *way!* Potty!" Tommy hobbled to the bathroom doorway. He was wearing one boot, a shredded black sock on his other foot. "Dawn Books out here wants me to play his sucking wedding!"

"No I don't. I just wanted to know if you had any sug—"

"How long has it been since I've played a wedding, Potty? Think about it, man. I play sucking *stadiums!*"

Stadia, Oscar thought helplessly. "I know. I don't—"

"I played at the sucking Berlin *Wall,* man! Boom!" There were yells of approval from the bathroom. Tommy turned away for a moment and spoke into the tape recorder in his hand: "Berlin Wall. Shopping mall. Had to fall. Something like that." He clicked the machine off. Clicked it back on. "See if we can fit it in before the chorus of 'Vomitoria.'"

"I didn't mean it as an insult," Oscar said. "I didn't even mean— I just wanted to get your advice." He shrugged, lifting and lowering his shoulder bag. "About bands."

A jagged coughing fit bent Tommy Gunn in half. "Bands," he said when he'd recovered. "Shit, I can talk bands with you. I can talk bands all night."

"It doesn't have to be all night." This was the night, after all, that he had to deliver the *Clog!* tickets to Kirk Connolly. "I just have to arrange the music for this

wedding, and thought you might have a few ideas. I
was kind of stuck for someone to ask."

"Got a show downtown tonight. Place called the
Fleshpot."

"Is that a club?"

"Kind of an S and M joint," he said. "Old hangout
of mine in the meat packing district. Join us?"

"I can't tonight. But thanks. Could I take a rain
check?"

He swept the top of his dresser and handed Oscar
a fan of tickets. "There you go. Be playing the
Fleshpot for the next couple weeks. Then I'm off on
tour with those pansies from Aerosmith." He wandered about the wreckage of food, laundry, and car
racing magazines. "Take a ride with me. Talk bands on
the way." He flopped, maybe fell, on the floor. "Just
need my other boot. *Das boot*, if you follow." He was
looking under the bed. "Help me look?"

"Sure."

"Look up high. I need you to look high. Because of
your—you know."

"Height," said Oscar.

"Call it what you will."

"Isn't that it right over there? In the punch bowl?"

Across the room was a large crystal bowl of bright
red liquid, a black toe visible in its center like an evil
crouton.

Tommy got to his feet. "Ma-a-a-an. Yes it is."

"Is that room service? I didn't know you could get
an entire bowl of punch delivered."

"Hey Dawn." He retrieved the dripping boot. "This is New York City. I am Tommy Sucking Gunn." He jerked it on and moved toward the door, squelching every other step. "I can get whatever I want."

By the time they had shouldered past the teenage Tommy Gunn fans who'd assembled by the elevators and the elderly tourists who cringed at the hotel entrance, their entourage included not only the former inhabitants of the bathroom — Potty in a toga, a woman in a pink raincoat, Cruller in a sleeveless T-shirt reading DEATH BY LETHAL ERECTION — but also a fat kid with black lipstick whom no one had ever seen before. Outside, the late-autumn light had turned a deeper blue and nearly vanished. They filed into a custom stretch limousine whose square grill and wood paneling suggested a frumpier former life as a plain old Jeep Wagoneer.

"You fit okay?" Tommy asked.

"No problem," Oscar said beside him. "This is the largest vehicle I've ever seen." The chauffeur closed the door and jogged around to the distant driver's seat. Several people on the sidewalk had formed pistols of their thumbs and forefingers and were waving them over their heads, chanting "Tom-my-Gunn! Tom-my-Gunn!"

"Get outta here, Dawn. You've been in limos before."

"I've ordered them," he said. "Every day. But never sat in one."

"Didn't you go to the sucking *prom*?"

"Actually, no."

"Formal dances and shit? Must've gone to college."

"Yes. But—no."

"Jake!" Tommy yelled up through the den area and over the dozen banks of seats. "To the Fleshpot!" The driver nodded and pulled out. Tommy swayed as the car bore hard right and he slid open the compartment over his armrest. He pulled out a glass decanter of something pale. The other passengers bayed and cursed. The woman in the pink raincoat was administering to the stereo across the car. Oscar counted nine Tommy Gunn albums in the rack of CDs to her left.

"Dawn?"

"No thanks. Really."

"Be my guest. Be it. Be my guest." He had filled a glass and was pushing it at him. "You're my guest. So be my guest."

"Well, I *have* had a lousy day." Oscar took the drink, spilling a bit as they changed lanes, full steam down Seventh Avenue. He watched as Tommy poured another glass.

"Happy Thanksgiving," he offered, and raised his glass toward Tommy's.

"Bam."

Oscar braced himself, steadying the beverage, and threw it back. But the liquid was sweet. "This is lemonade."

"When life gives you limos," said Tommy, "make limo-nade."

And just like that, things got better. Oscar stretched out his legs as far as they would go. Even crossed them, luxuriously. He watched the buildings slide by and the population scatter at the crosswalks, making way. *Dear Lauren,* he thought. *It is with regret that I acknowledge the misconception*—too formal. *Lauren,* he started again. *I can't help but wish I'd told you*—double negative. He reached into his shoulder bag to find a piece of paper. He dragged out his binder, now crammed with papers and pamphlets. The tickets to tomorrow's Tommy Gunn show fell into his lap as well.

"On Thanksgiving we *killll,*" the singer was growling into his handheld tape recorder. "And then eat our *fillll.*"

Oscar smiled as he clicked off. "Now," he said, "about bands."

"Bands!" Tommy shouted, which started him coughing. He hit a few buttons over his head and the CD player jumped on, causing the woman in the pink raincoat to fall back and clap. He fast-forwarded, with a crashing series of first chords and opening notes, to one of his loud and popular ballads that sounded as if it might have something to do with love. "There you go!" he yelled over the whomp of the bass. "There's your wedding song! Bam!" He pressed another button and an oversized television screen opened ten yards in front of them. He zipped through several crooked-lined music videos before slowing at the sight of Billy Idol snarling the chorus of *White Wedding*. "There you have it," he said. "Ye-e-e-e-eah. Billy rules."

They rode like that for a few blocks, watching one song and listening to another, audiovisually overloaded and all nodding to different beats. Tommy, when he spoke, had to slump close to Oscar to be heard.

Call concert promoters, comb liner notes, scour the pages at the back of music magazines and the bulletin boards in front of music schools; but the best way to find a band is by ear. Boom. Rock 'n' roll tends to muddle after an hour or so. Reggae lopes into boredom. But swing can jump-start the joint, samba loosens the hips, and Motown inspires even the oldies to ratchet up from their chairs and buckle a knee or two. Bam. Think klezmer, ponder zydeco, consider mariachi, go for all three. Deejays can save you a sucking fortune; just be sure to screen their collections in advance. Synthesizers are cheaper than extra musicians, although the imitation brass section tends to be weak. Plan on four hours of music, twenty amps of electricity. Check on risers and lighting and the timing of the meal.

"How do you know all this?"

"I played weddings." He was examining his lemonade as if it were fine wine. "I played a suck of a lot of weddings."

"But you never had one yourself."

"Never got around to it. Always meant to," he said. "Just never, you know. Meant to." He scratched his stubbly chin. "You'll read about that in the book." He looked ahead to the other seats and gave the fat kid the thumbs-up. Stuck his tongue way out and waggled it, possibly rehearsing for the show.

"So what does a guy like Tommy Gunn do for Thanksgiving?" Oscar asked. "Take a bath in Wild Turkey? Bite the head off a sweet potato?"

"Home to Jersey. Mom, stepdad, sister. Tofu turkey."

"Seriously?"

"I don't eat creatures." He patted his ribbed stomach. "No meat, no booze. Secret of my success. Boom. That'll be in the book."

"No, I mean Jersey," Oscar said. "I'm from New Jersey."

"Everybody's from New Jersey." He looked out the window. "One way or another." He glugged the last of his drink. "So what does a guy like Dawn Books do for Thanksgiving?"

"He works."

"No-o-o-o-o."

"It's no big deal," he said. "I'll go to New Jersey for a late dinner. Whip up something for my dad."

"Where's your mom?"

"She died. Long time ago."

"Bites," said Tommy. "No bros or sisses?"

"Nope."

"Don't got a girlie?"

"No gir— Well, there is someone. Yes." He reached over to pour himself another lemonade. He was smiling goofily, drunk on his answer. He took a sip and sobered up. "I'm working on it, anyway."

"There you go."

"Screwing it up as we speak."

Potty climbed back over a seat. Punched him on the knee. "Girlie problems?"

"Ow. You could say that."

"Gimme the problem."

"It's nothing," said Oscar. He jerked backward as Jake decided to run the light. "It's complicated."

"Give Potty the problem," Tommy encouraged. "Give it up, Dawn. Give of yourself. Potty can take it."

"You got two girlies," Potty guessed. The toga had fallen open around his gut. "Don't you."

"No. Well, in effect, yes. Ironically."

"I-whatally?"

"And you're about to get married," Tommy jumped in. "Bam."

"I'm not getting married. One of them is getting married. Although I don't think she should."

"That's because you got a thing for her. Boom."

"No, I have a thing for the other girlie. Woman. Who thinks that *I'm* getting married. Which I'm not. Not unless she wants to," he added. "Which she does." He sipped from his glass. "She just doesn't want to plan it."

The two men looked drained.

"Forget it."

"Ma-a-a-a-an." Tommy held up his tape recorder. "That's a song."

"No doubt," Potty agreed.

"What is."

"Say it again, Dawn. Sing it into here."

"I don't sing," Oscar said.

"Everybody sings," said Tommy. "Just think up some words. You're into words. Take a minute, write them down, and then let loose. I'll have it burned onto a CD for you."

"You can do that?"

"Add some guitar and a drum beat, easy enough. Half hour in the studio. You with me, Potty?"

Oscar shrugged and ripped out a blank piece of paper. "It's kind of *for* somebody. Is that all right?"

"That's a song," Potty told him.

With the steady encouragement and bellowed contributions of the other passengers, Oscar got something down and croaked it, with backup, into the recorder. When the session was a wrap, Tommy asked him, "So where are we dropping you?"

"Jane Street, please."

He had taken out the Dawn Books envelope containing the Dawn Books stationery on which he'd written Dawn's note. He pulled out the old tickets, inserted the new. On the television screen a woman in a bodystocking was making love to the microphone stand while three men with long perms ruined their instruments behind her.

"You want this girl, Dawn? I can get her for you."

Oscar laughed. "That's all right."

"She'll do a wedding," said Tommy. "I'll tell her to do your wedding."

"I think I'd better keep looking. Thank you."

"You should come to the show tonight. Lot of musicians there. Tell me which one you want and I'll make it happen."

"I'm afraid I can't. I have an errand to—"

But a cacophony of objections rose from the rest of the limousine. Cruller threw a CD at him that he barely deflected aside. The woman in the raincoat groveled on the floor with her arms cinching his legs. Potty was pretending to sob.

"Okay. You know what? I want to come. I'll come."

"Bam! There you go!" Tommy shouted over the victorious whistles and blaring music.

"Can I just drop something off on the way?"

"Say the word, Dawn."

Oscar called ahead: "Jane Street, Jake."

They parked alongside four cars and a UPS truck. The block was postcard-pretty, featuring actual trees and a tweeting bird that might have been hired by the hour. Through his window Oscar watched Potty and Cruller add themselves to the setting. After swearing and wrestling over the envelope, Potty emerged triumphant with it held between his teeth. The two zigzagged up the stone steps of the town house. Cruller lifted and dropped the brass battleship that adorned the front door. Potty kicked him from behind, and Cruller shoved him back and almost off the stoop as the door groaned open.

He was wearing a leather flight jacket, his slacks freshly pressed. Aviator sunglasses shone against the tropical tan of his skin. On the whole, Kirk Connolly looked a lot like his back-jacket author photos, if decidedly shorter than when posed on the deck of an aircraft carrier or positioned in the foreground with missile silos on the distant horizon. He received the wet letter between two fingers and watched the pair retreat to the limo, knocking fists and slamming the gate on their way. His face had puckered into the manful squint of his main characters as they oversaw the explosion of Iranian embassies, the arc of atomic warheads a few minutes from Red Square. This was an author who—like Oscar—knew the importance of plotting events, of the daring twists and ugly scenes necessary to pull off a happy ending.

By contrast, the expression on the faces of Cruller and Potty was sheer joy when Oscar offered them, as payment for their service, two front-row tickets to *Clog!*

The Registry

THE CHRISTMASES SHE SPENT at home were easier, she thought. A stocking from Mom, breakfast in bed, a few days of peace on earth—or at least in Idaho—before she was off once again to write about all the good little girls and boys who got what they wanted: a Santa Claus wedding in Michigan, a New Year's Eve ceremony in New Mexico. In New York, however, the street corners were the clanging battleground of the Salvation Army, jingle bells every-

where like the sound of prisoners shambling in chains.
The ferocious smell of chestnuts, unpurchased by
absolutely anyone ever and all the stronger for it. Not
to mention the inevitable blizzard of cards.

"Those are from the magazine," she told Chris,
who was poking at the sliding pile of them on her
kitchen counter. "They forward my Christmas cards.
Hanukkah and Kwanza too."

"These are all greeting cards?" Chris picked up a
handful and let them drop and scatter.

"Not greetings. Invitations. *My fiancée and I are
planning to be wed in an igloo north of Juno this January.
Would you be willing to strap on a seal skin and write our
story?*"

"Come on."

"Green envelope there, with the Alaska stamp. Or
check out the red one by the sink. *My fiancée and I are
to be married this February on a luge run in Aspen. Our speed
at the time we exchange the rings should approach a hundred
miles an hour. We trust that you can see the appeal of such an
ev —*"

"Incredible." She cleared aside a drapery of
Lauren's bras to sit down in her broken easy chair.

"Don't you hate the word *fiancée?* There's something irritating about it. I don't think it's just me. It's
the word. *Fiancée. Fiancée.*" Lauren walked to her filmy
window and made an effort to see out. A musical car
horn tooted the first five notes of "Feliz Navidad."

"What's that one?" Chris pointed to the top of a
mound among the many other mounds in the apart-

ment. "The square one. It looks like a CD. People will try anything, huh." She reached for the small package and dropped back in the chair. "Hey, this is from Oscar. As in *Oscar?*"

"Have a listen." Lauren took the CD from her and crossed the room toward her stereo.

Chris was reading the package. "It came from the magazine. Doesn't he have your address? We're talking about the same Oscar here."

"Nobody has my address. You ready for this?" She pressed Play and turned up the volume. After a screaming guitar opening and four stomps of a bass drum, it was —haltingly, yet unmistakeably —Oscar.

"If love is a book / then I wrote the wrong beginning: / a false start / a dull part / that you'd be better off skimming / to reach the heart of the story / where the plot thickens, starring you. / If I had more main character, / I'd have begun on page one with the truth."

At which point the guitar took over, along with the shrieks of other people. Chris winced through another two verses. Toward the end it sounded as if someone was smashing something fragile —which is where Lauren hit it off.

Chris uncovered her ears. "So he's not getting married. It's not him. It's his freaking boss."

"You got it."

"That's great."

"Think so?" Lauren moved to her kitchen cabinet, pulled out and shook an empty cereal box, and put it back.

"Sure I think so. This whole time you were convinced he was engaged. And he's not. He's single.
Available."

"I don't think it's so great," she said. "I think it's
typical."

"Typical?"

"Typical of men. You remember men. Think back,
Chris. Let me remind you how men work." She
smacked her palm with the back of her hand. "They
hide behind things. Bury themselves in projects.
Duck under their big doings, so that they don't have
to own up to any real feelings or take a chance on
something that could actually change their lives.
Men," she said, "do not act like men. They don't
brave things. They don't *do* things. Men are . . . boys."

"Lost me there."

"He lied to me," she said.

"No, he didn't. You assumed incorrectly, and he
just didn't bother to set you straight. He couldn't, like
the song says. He didn't have a choice."

"He did, though. There's always a choice. The
truth is always a choice." Her voice wavered. "*I* was a
choice. And he didn't take it. Me."

"Well, he gave you his phone number." She held
up the liner notes from the inside of the CD box.

"I already had his phone number."

"So you should call him."

"No chance."

"Why not? He doesn't have your number. Or your
address. He has no way—"

"You call him," she snapped. "I'm tired of groveling at every opportunity, of lowering my standards every time a guy disappoints me. Especially this guy. This guy's not disappointing." She leaned over Chris to collect her bras from behind her shoulder and throw them at her bedroom. "At least I didn't think so."

"You should call him, Lauren."

"I'm not going to call him."

"You're in love with him."

"I'm not calling."

"Suit yourself."

Lauren went back to the window. She pressed her forehead to the glass. "I have to get out of this city."

There came the Yuletide serenade of the Spanish car horn. *Feliz Navidad, Feliz Navidad*—loud enough to obscure the complaints of the easy chair as Chris leaned sideways and pushed the liner notes into the front pocket of her jeans.

To be a person's assistant is to be no one at all. He dwelled between people, drifted among them without quite existing. He sent faxes for Marion, passed along the comments of Carl, rendered and delivered the verdicts of Dawn. He didn't actually matter; he only helped other people to do so. But that wasn't what was bothering him. He had sent the CD to Lauren and heard nothing back. He had tried again to get her number from the magazine and gotten nowhere. So it was over. He'd ruined it. This was what he deserved, this eternal drudgery for others. A three-course, four-appetizer, five-hundred-guested labor of lovelessness that he had two months to ruin as well.

By early December most storefronts and apartment lobbies are downright depressing, having smothered the occasion in coats of red and gobs of white, in eight candles and nine reindeer and uncountable numbers of streamers and signs. Carl's office was even sadder than that due to the absolute lack thereof. Empty of accessories, it stank only of sweat and paper: of the death, by slices, of hundreds of trees, and of the slower demise of the man in their midst.

"We still on?" Oscar asked him from the doorway.

"Indeed."

"I appreciate it, Carl. I know shopping isn't exactly your cup of tea."

"On the contrary, my boy: it is *your* cup of tea that we are after. Among other things. 'Tis the season," he said tartly, "for *things*."

"That's the spirit."

"For slapdash capitalism. Ribald consumerism."

"Ho, ho, ho."

"Has Dawn left the building?" Carl asked. "I felt a distinct lightening of the floor beams and girders, a cease in the tremble of the foundations, some few minutes past."

"She's at lunch. We'll go in a minute. I just have to return one phone call."

He ducked back into the hallway. Pulled the message slip from his pocket. Ordinarily he would hurry;

but lately he had no interest. In fact, in this case, with this caller, it was in his interest—or at least hers—to stall. At his desk he spent some time rotating his tin of Christmas cookies until they faced exactly outward.

"Darling Oscar."

"Maid Marion."

She strutted before him. "I've just been reading the most astounding piece of literature." She held it behind her back.

"That we're publishing? That is astounding."

"Sheesh. What's wrong with you?"

"Nothing," he said. "What's the book?"

"You've been a real wet blanket for the past couple weeks. It's not like you." She shimmied closer. "Wedding still on?"

"Unfortunately."

"Well, aren't you the romantic fool. Maybe this will inspire you. I believe you're familiar with the author's work. She writes under the name"—she threw down a magazine—"of Loose Lips LaRose."

His legs clenched. It was the Maine column: a full-page photograph of the hill and ocean, a corner insert of the couple of the month. Wendy looked radiant, her veil not quite veiling the bunny-ears being held overhead by an unpictured Ken or Steve. On the facing page, the pull-out quote in large crimson lettering was Oscar's.

"It's not enough to fall in love," Marion recited by heart, hands folded beneath her chest like a contestant in a spelling bee. *"You have to pick yourself up and do something about it."*

"All right."

"Oscar Campbell, 31, a college friend of the groom's."

"Okay, Marion. You've had your fun."

"But you know what? Her writing's gotten better. A bit. If you read closely." She looked down, considering the cookies. "So does she look like what I think she looks like? Beehive hairdo? Kind of an old hen?"

"She's not old."

"So more of a dumpy little cupcake," she said. She blew air into her cheeks.

"Not dumpy, no."

"Did you keep in touch? I don't think she lives in New York."

"She does. We did."

"Wait till your fiancée reads—"

"And then we didn't," he said. "Listen, I have to make a call."

"You're famous, Oscar. 'Aisle of White.'"

"Dream come true," he said. "Do you mind if I make a call?" He put his hand on the phone.

"Women are going to be all over you for this. Everybody reads 'Aisle of White.' I could definitely get you a date with that model. Remember that model I was telling you about?"

"She's not a model," he said. "She's a *hand* model. You said it yourself."

"That's modeling. I could call her right now. She's probably already read the piece."

"No. Thank you."

But she didn't leave. Casually her eyes roved his

desk. A flicker of eyebrows when she caught sight of Gordon Fox's name on the message slip. "Still chatting with our friend Fox, I see."

"Afraid so." He jiggled the phone in its cradle. "It's crunch time on *Global Intrusion.* Which is why I really have to c—"

"What a sleaze."

"Who, Gordon?" He took his hand from the phone. "Tell me about it."

"Wish I could," she said. "Sworn to secrecy."

"You have dirt on Gordy?"

"Me? Dirt?"

He stood up behind his desk. "Out with it, Marion."

"Sorry, sweetie."

"I beg you. Give me one thing. A name. A place. Anything I can use."

"What do you mean *use.* Use for what?"

"*Lose.* I said *lose.* Anything I can lose. As soon as you tell me, it's lost. Goes nowhere." He shrugged and sat back down. "I'm just curious."

She looked back down the hallway. Took a cookie. "I'll give you a name. No," she decided, "not a name."

"Come on. A name."

"I'll give you a position."

"Yuck."

"Not that kind of position." She peeked around again. "Sub-rights assistant," she confided. "HarperCollins."

"Leah? I know Leah. He's been with Leah? She's like twenty-one years old."

"I'm not saying. Could be. Could have been two nights ago. And last week?" She ran a hand through her flaming hair, warming up. "Associate publisher. Simon and Schuster."

"With Beth? That's repulsive. Poor Beth."

"Poor senior editor at Morrow. As long as you're handing out condolences. Say a prayer for the junior publicist at Holt. Personally, I feel for the production manager at Viking. Three weeks ago. Seattle Book Fair. Caught her alone in the hotel swimming pool."

"But you don't have any, um"—he shrugged again— "proof."

"Proof? The man is a rabid wolf. Everyone knows it. Why do you need proof?"

"I don't. There's just . . . nothing in writing, in other words. Nothing to show anyone. Like pictures. Letters. Skin samples."

"You think I need visual aids to get my info?"

"It's not tha—"

"You think my sources aren't reliable?"

"I'm sure they are," he said quickly.

But she was off in a huff, her slander having been slandered; angrier than he'd ever seen her when criticized on matters of book publicity. Alone at last, he read the magazine. Closed it sadly. Punched it furiously. Then he inserted it into his bag. He dialed the phone and was banished into voice mail, rescued and told to wait, instructed to call back, and finally patched through.

"O? That you?"

"It's me, Gordy. You called?"

"I called you over an hour ago. What the hell's going on over there?" He was typing as he spoke: Oscar could hear the heavy tap dance of his fingers on the keys.

"What do you need?"

"Wrong, pal. I'm calling because of what *you* need."

"And what's that."

"Not what. Who. Kirk Connolly is who. Problem is, I don't think you people know how bad you need him. 'Cause I'll tell you, he's not happy."

"He's not." Oscar tried to keep the satisfaction from his voice.

"Dawn gave him tickets to some sicko fuckfest and the guy almost got shoved in a dumpster. The man was *appalled*." It was an unnatural word for Gordon Fox, and he struggled with the inflection. "So *I'm* appalled. And you know what happens when I'm appalled."

"I don't."

"I yank someone. I pull my author and I put him somewhere else. For me it's like—what do you call those balls. Those silver balls you move around in your hand."

"Huh."

"That's what it's like. I move things around and I feel better. Hold for me, buddy."

The Muzak was a spunky rendition of "Bridge over Troubled Water." Oscar was humming along and putting on his parka when Gordy returned.

"If I have to yank my main man," he said, "I yank myself. And I think the old gal would miss me if I was to disappear with my man. I think she'd rather I was *around*, in the near future. Like, say, mid-March. If you know what I mean."

"I do."

"You do what. Whatcha going to do, Big O. Wait—let me get Marcy." There was the gravelly sound of an intercom. "Marce! Don't move. Oscar's going to make us happy. Go on, O-Dog. You were telling us how you're gonna save the day."

"I'll, um, come up with something," he said. One more foul-up, he thought. Another wrench thrown into the publishing process ought to bring the wedding to a halt as well. If he didn't have the proof to scare Dawn off the marriage, then he would just have to make Gordy yank himself instead.

"You will, won't you. That's what I thought. 'Cause you're the man. The man with the plan. Marce! Hear that? Big O's gonna come up with something. So don't move. Actually—move, Marcy. Go get me something. A sandwich. No, a half sandwich. Two half sandwiches. Got that? With— Oscar? Kid?"

"I'm right here."

"What kind of sandwich do I want? Think fast. Whatcha got for me on the sandwich."

The other line lit like a beacon: his line.

"I have to go."

"I'm thinking soppressata. With mozzarella. On focaccia. You there?"

"I have to answer the phone."

"Don't leave me hanging, O. I'm a hungry man. And you're the man with the plan. I'm thinking I could use a—"

He pressed the other button.

"Hello, Dawn Books."

"Oscar."

"Can I help you?" he asked.

"Do you have a pen?"

"Who's this."

"My name's Chris."

"Chris from ICM?"

"No."

"From William Morris. Right. We owe you contracts," he said. "Dawn's been so busy—"

"Chris Lucas."

"Oh."

There was no sound for a moment.

"Are you a hand model?"

"What? No. I have an address to give you. Her address. Before I change my mind. Just don't tell her it was me."

"Tell who? Tell her it was who?"

"Exactly," said Chris. "Now take this down."

The department store a few blocks from the office had decked its halls in paper products, faux snow fogging all the windows. To Oscar it seemed a generous helping of cheer, sprayed and dangled by good-hearted companies for the enjoyment of eager-eyed kids. Dreamy with gratitude, he could have given out holiday hugs to everyone on line between him and the fourth-floor bridal registry counter. It was the season for Chrises — Kringle, Lucas — to come through. It was his day.

Even Carl seemed rather jolly when Oscar confessed: "This registering thing feels a bit presumptuous. I'm essentially ordering people to buy me something expensive."

"Nonsense," came the answer. "You are making *order* of the *expensive* things that people will purchase for you in any event."

"Damned copy editors." He smiled. "Always switching your words around on you."

A customer stood off a few yards to the right of the line, typing information into what appeared to be a slot machine. She reached down to remove something from a tray, and Oscar thought for a moment that this was how one got gifts from a registry: that she would lift a silver platter or crystal vase from the dispenser, having hit the jackpot, and take it home. But she departed with a mere piece of paper, and he faced forward to watch a couple take possession of a dangerous-looking mechanism and be sent on their way.

"What's that?" he whispered to Carl.

"My word. It looks like a gun."

They reached the head of the line. Carl was peering nervously at the droves of shoppers, the sparkling flatware, the glints off the glassware that beckoned and attacked them from all sides. Oscar imagined that

the man hadn't mingled with the population and mer-
chandise of the city like this for years. He was fiddling
with the buttons of his shirt as if one of them, pressed
in time, might beam him back to his desk.

"You okay, Carl?"

"Certainly."

They stepped forward to greet the saleswoman in
a starched blouse behind the counter. She typed in
Oscar's full name and address and the date of the
occasion. She paused, fingers twitching, after asking
the bride's. With a quick look at Carl he promised to
phone in that information as soon as possible. It didn't
matter, he thought, to the two frowns of concern
before and beside him. There would be no wedding,
no presents, if all went according to plan. Grudgingly
the woman handed over a large calculator with a plastic handle. "Just zap and go," she explained. "Aim
and press the trigger until the red line has read the
bar code. When it beeps, the item's automatically
entered on your registry. And you two are all set." She
gave them a well-rehearsed prenuptial blessing, a
you-two-will-be-great-together smile of approval,
which petered out uncomfortably as she watched the
two men head off.

Oscar pointed the weapon forward, arms straight,
knees bent. "Stay behind me," he commanded.

"Oscar. Really."

"Shhht!" He brought the gun up, two-handed,
beside his head. He froze for a beat before turning the
corner. "Stick close, Carl."

"Come now."

He dropped the routine as they faced the glimmering assembly of goblets and flutes. There were pilsners and decanters, old-fashioneds and double old-fashioneds, beer mugs and highballs and cordials.

"What do you drink?" Carl prompted. "Or rather, what *will* you drink? That's the crux of it, my boy. You must imagine your life together."

Oscar shut his eyes to imagine it. It was so easy to picture her, to envision them together. And there was her face. And a kitchen—and then a whole house—around that. It unfolded as from a kit: the yard, the town, the life, all bundled somehow beneath her surface, coiled to spring from the lights in her eyes.

"You'll drink brandy, I presume."

When he looked, Carl was holding a snifter by its stem.

"In which case these will be of some use."

"I've never tried brandy," Oscar admitted. "I could start. Do husbands drink brandy?"

Thoughtfully Carl rubbed his slick upper lip. "I believe that they do."

"Then so will I." He aimed the gun at the sticker on the base of the glass and pulled the trigger. A laser-line of red appeared and he dragged it across the bar code. *Doop.* "Hey, it worked. Now number of items."

"Twelve."

"Really?"

"One gets twelve."

He tapped the numbers on the miniature keyboard. "I knew I could use your advice. What else."

Carl turned, arms open, to embrace the rest of the store. "What else indeed."

If it seems crass, my boy, then blame the stores; for a registry is nothing more than a ploy for your shopping loyalty from the get-go. Nothing less than a haul. Announce a hankering for a pierced tablespoon or three-foot pepper mill and watch it magically appear in the evolving comfort of your home. Make certain your gifts will be stocked in time for the bridal shower, discounted after the wedding day, exchangeable without a fuss. National chains are convenient for out-of-towners. Home improvement centers are ideal for do-it-yourselfers. Resist the electric mixer the size of a tow truck, the gravy boat the price of a Boston Whaler. Go for decent knives and durable towels, nonstick pans and a toaster you can trust. And enjoy the brand-new feeling of wealth that comes with love, and of love that comes with wealth, as you prepare for a little of both to enter your life and be unwrapped and incorporated.

"Wait up." It was hard to limp forward while taking notes in the binder. "This is helpful. Carl?"

They moved into the country of china, the older man in the lead. "Ah, the finery," he exclaimed before shelves of white circles and squares.

"Look at you," Oscar marveled.

"I am a gentleman, like any other gentleman, who has always enjoyed the impeccable clap of a cup in a saucer."

A picture of Carl emerged, a moving picture that

told the story of his long-ago empire being over-thrown by the thudding clubs of barbarians on his palace door at teatime. He had been ransacked and dethroned, sentenced to copyedit for nincompoops, entombed in a vulgar house with no appreciation for the olden days. Life depended on luck—love, too, was luck—and a single phone call, a mumbled address, could improve your chances in an instant. Or else, Oscar thought, the call never comes. He regarded the man twirling before the fruit saucers with sudden affection.

"Tell me what to shoot, Carl."

"So many choices," he said. "Waterford. Wedgwood. Mikasa. Royal Worcester."

"Just point." Oscar sighted over his wrist, narrowed an eye. "At anything. Twenty bucks says I can hit it from here."

"And the patterns. Isabella. Tennyson. Amherst. Cornucopia. Stoneleigh. Lockleigh."

"*Quick*-ly," he said. "I've got an itchy trigger finger."

"Hoorah. Jacobean." He pointed, magisterially, to a floral-edged soup bowl on the top shelf. "Can you reach it?"

Oscar rose, eyeing the target, rose higher, and squeezed. *Doop.*

"Ya-ha!" Carl clutched his arm. "*Strange things I have in head, that will to hand, / Which must be acted ere they will be scanned!* Macbeth. Act three, scene four."

"Twelve of these, you think?"

"Lovely Jacobean. Playful, seasonal, sophisticated."

"Fine. Twenty-four. Thirty-six." He typed in thirty-six. "If I didn't know better, I'd say you were having fun."

"I am, I am." Carl had taken off his glasses to rub his eyes. He wasn't as old as he seemed when saddled with his hokey eyewear. "Weddings, to be sure, are meant to be fun."

"I thought you were against marriage."

"Marriage?" he blustered. "I know nothing of marriage."

"You once told me the world can be divided into workers and—"

"The world," he said sternly, putting back on his spectacles, "is divided enough as it is."

Oscar shot behind-the-back at strainers. Across the store at microwaves. Between the legs at a waffle iron, missing and nailing an innocent breadmaker instead. A shopping trip for household goods is the frontier for engaged men: a gold-rush settlement of outlaws and in-laws where you learn fast, take whatever you can get, and shoot anything that moves you before your patience is shot first.

"I'm about done," he said.

"Take heart, boy. We're almost to cutlery."

"It's after two o'clock." That left him forty-five minutes to get downtown and back up to the office, having gotten the chance to talk to Lauren and straighten out what he couldn't in song. He was standing before a display of cheese boards, cutting boards, and carving boards. Wearily he shot two of each. "Let's call it a day."

"I say we persevere. Crock pots, Oscar. Hand blenders. Rice cookers."

"And *I* say"—he pointed the gun, now, at Carl—"you turn around *very slowly* and walk out the door with me, partner. That's it. Real natural-like."

"Casseroles! You haven't a single—"

"Move it."

Carl trudged in front of him, the plastic gun jammed into his back. "You'll regret this," he said.

"Not another word, hombre."

"Without a casserole dish, you will be unable—"

"Into the elevator. That's it."

"But you haven't returned the—"

"Shhht!"

"Very well."

On the way downtown he shot himself a brownstone, two Labrador retrievers, an orange pylon (accidentally), a handheld cup of coffee (impressively), and a two-hundred-dollar haircut from an upper-crust salon. In the blink of an eye he owned his own Greek restaurant. Sighting out the window of his taxi, he could not be denied. This was New York Sucking City; he could have whatever he wanted. He could be a stockbroker, a greengrocer. He could change neighborhoods, abandon his career. Zap and go to a different state, start his life again—or start another one—in a place he'd never seen. He had, he realized, better things to do. He blew on the end of the gun and put it away. Looked again at her address as the cab dropped him off.

Her building was a chipped heap of bricks between a Dominican family planning center and the manufacturer of tombstone monuments on the corner. Trapped, he thought fondly, between other people's beginnings and endings. He pressed a buzzer that didn't sound as if it worked. Rapped on the lobby door. Stepping back onto the sidewalk, he gazed upward into a fluttering line of laundry strung from the fire escape to a No Parking sign. A window was jockeyed open on the ground floor.

"Sorry to bother you," he told the woman in the denim jacket at the sill. "I was looking for Lauren in Two-B."

"Lauren? She's gone."

"Gone?"

"Well, not yet. Soon, though."

"What do you mean?" He stepped toward her. "Are you Chris, by any chance?"

"I'm Svenya," she said. "I'll get Chris."

She disappeared for a minute. A black-haired woman came into view. "So you're Oscar."

"I am. Thanks for calling."

"Lauren had some meeting at the magazine. Turning something in, trimming something down."

"I should have figured," he said. "I just wanted to come by right away."

"Is that a gun?"

"This?" He patted his waistband. "No, it's just a— Do you know when she'll be back?"

"That's a tough one," she said. "She's heading off

tomorrow morning to some wedding in Wisconsin. Then Virginia. Then maybe Montana. I forget the order. Thirteen, I think she said, in the next couple months. She won't be back until March."

"Why?"

"They're making her stockpile a year's worth of articles to run after she leaves. I guess the column's so popular that they've got to keep—"

"Leaves?" he asked.

Chris lowered her elbows onto the windowsill. "She's taking off. I didn't tell you that part. That's why I had to call you."

"Taking off for where?"

"Back home. Iowa. Ohio."

"Idaho," he said. "When?"

"As soon as she gets all her columns done. March. Sooner if she can."

"I don't believe it." He paced a few steps. Stamped a shoe on the pavement. "I don't *believe* it."

"So I hear you're not getting married."

He squinted down the street. "I'm never getting married."

"Me neither," she said.

"She's really leaving."

"Wouldn't you?"

"I would. Yes. I would leave," he said.

"She thinks you're not willing to take a chance on her."

"A chance? What does she— But I am."

"You are?"

"Completely. Absolutely."

"So prove it."

"Prove it?" He looked around. "How?"

"I don't know. Find a way," she said. "Take a chance."

"Right." He paced again. "That's right." A way. A chance. He pulled out the gun and twirled it on his finger, walking and thinking harder. Slowly something began to sprout, the way the weeds at his feet were sprouting bravely through the leftover snow on the sidewalk. It gripped his chest, flowered in his head. But that was crazy. But that was what she'd told him: she just wanted to walk in. He took another few steps. But he could never make it happen, he thought. But of course he could. The wheels of the wedding were already in motion. All he needed was to make sure they came off.

Chris was about to close the window when his head jerked up.

"I'm putting together this wedding in March," he told her.

"I know."

"And I'd like to invite Lauren to come cover it. For the magazine."

"Get in line," she laughed. "Have you seen how many letters she gets?"

"But this is perfect for 'The Aisle of White.' There's a book theme."

"Come again?"

"Books. It's all about books. There'll be famous

authors, big-name publishers—do you know Tommy Gunn?"

"Never heard of him."

"You've never heard of Tommy Gunn? The rock star? The heavy metal—never mind. Kirk Connolly will be there. The writer. You know Kirk Connolly."

"Haven't had the pleasure," she said. "But I'll ask her for you."

"Lauren? You will? Thank you. That would be great. Just ask. The wedding's March sixteenth. I'll send her an invitation." He smiled. "You should come too. If you're not busy."

"I'll think about it."

"I can't believe you've never heard of Kirk Connolly," he said. "Don't you go to the movies? Have you been locked away in a monastery?"

"You could say that."

"What do you do?"

Chris told him what she did.

He tapped the gun against his chin. "You don't say."

The Invitations

THE MAN'S NAKED CHEST bouldered out from an unbuttoned shirt. The woman clawed at his pantaloons, swooning onto the tall grass of the plantation. Farmhouse, cliff: the usual. Not particularly different from the cover of last year's *Kiss in Kansas*, minus the cows. A lot like *Never in Nebraska* without the corn. Oscar stared at the image on the computer screen.

"We'd better hurry."

"I am," he said.

But there was something in those Technicolor meadows that drew him in, that welcomed and waved to him with a thousand golden hands. He was from New Jersey. His chest would never look anything like that. Still, he could almost feel the warmth of a western sun, hear the laughing rasp of the fields.

"They're going to be back any second," Deborah persisted.

"Okay. Go ahead." He rolled back his chair to give her room to work. He watched her push a few keys, wiggle the mouse. She cast an apprehensive glance out the door of the design department.

"You want the title taken out, you said."

He nodded.

"And replaced with—what again?" She deleted *Moonlight in Missouri.*

"*Global Intrusion.*"

"Global what?"

"*Intrusion.*"

"What's *Global Intrusion*?"

"It's the title."

"But it doesn't make any sense."

"It's a thriller, Deborah. It's not supposed to make sense. You haven't spent much time in the editorial department, have you."

"Not yet."

"Well, we have a room on the other side of the building where we go in cases like this. In the Thriller

Room are two file cabinets: one full of adjectives, the other nouns. All we have to do is reach in and pull out one of each. They don't have to match; we're on deadline. *Final . . . Dagger.* Good enough. *Legal . . . Murder.* Will do. See, the trick—"

"We should really hurry," she said.

"You're right. Onward. *Global Intrusion.*"

She substituted the title in the same loopy purple script across a bale of hay. "Like that?"

"Perfect."

"What kind of trouble can I get in for this?"

"Don't worry," he said. "*Moonlight*'s already in production. The cover's done. Dawn's presenting the book next month at sales conference. As a matter of fact, the author's coming in today for her prelaunch pep talk. No one's going to reopen the file."

"I don't know." She took her hands from the keyboard.

"Deborah, you owe me," he said. "Who ran out and bought Dawn a new vase before she came back from her meeting?"

"I know. I just—"

"Who took the memo off her chair before she picked it up, crossed the building, and stuffed it down your throat?"

"That was you. Fine. Author." Resuming her manipulations, she deleted *Cherry Margaret* and typed in the new name as he spelled it. "You've got to be kidding," she said. "Kirk Connolly?"

"I know. It's a departure for him."

"I have a feeling this is going to be a departure for me."

"No, it's not. Nobody will know."

"Kirk Connolly will know."

"Oh, he's nobody," Oscar said. "You'll learn that."

He was only following orders, he thought. Dawn had demanded that he send the author his cover for approval. Gordy had insisted that his client be shown the design-in-progress as soon as possible. There were footsteps in the hall. They both froze at the sound— until one of the maintenance guys from four wandered by with a hammer. "So you'll be able to print this right away and messenger it to the address I gave you?"

"That's easy," she said.

"The mail room's on two," he said.

"I know that."

"And remember: This is top secret."

"You told me."

"And you know what that means. Top secret."

"Sure."

"Tell no one. Not your boss, not his boss, and not even her boss, who reports to Dawn. This is your project, Deborah. All you."

"Okay. Now, can I ask you—"

"Not me, Deborah. You. Soup to nuts. *You.*"

"I understand, Oscar. I just have to know—"

"Deborah!" He slapped his forehead. Then he caught himself. "I'm sorry. What were you asking?"

She looked again out the door before whispering, "Glossy or matte?"

A message slip was crushed and thrown at his head. Dawn mauled a memo from the sales department and tossed that Oscarward as well. He couldn't blame her, he thought, jackknifed into her guest chair and wincing at the projectiles as they passed. It felt good to ball up urgent notices and make them go away. He could still feel in his fingers the squash of the fax from Kirk Connolly concerning an evening at the Fleshpot, the tickle in his palm of Gordy's question about a dog track. The happy crunch of the news that no one was happy. Out her window it had started to snow.

"Cherry's in reception," he reminded her.

"What Cherry?"

"Cherry Margaret."

"Goddamn prima donna," she said. "If she yammers on too long, you buzz and tell me I have a meeting."

"No problem. I have to talk to her anyway."

"You? Why do *you* have to talk to her? She doesn't want to talk to you, Oscar."

"I like her," he objected.

"You would. Jesus. Prima donnas, both of you."

She jettisoned a red-penciled note from Carl. The snow was hitting the pane rapidly, almost audibly, like mouse punches.

"What's this?"

"That's the guest list."

"Oscar." She held up the packet of pages. "How many times—"

"For sales conference."

This quelled her momentarily. But then came the shift in the sharp angles of her face. "Since when do we have a guest list for sales conference?"

"Since, you know." He lowered his voice. "Since the same people will be attending another event immediately afterward. I was just wondering if there was anyone I should invite who wasn't already coming to the conference. Any . . . family, for example." He looked at her hopefully. "Or, say . . . friends." He checked her expression again. No friends.

She held the pages at arm's length. Then she tore them in half. In quarters. In eighths. She spread her empty hands as the scraps cascaded onto and off her desk, piling up whitely on the white rug as inevitably as snow.

"How goes the wedding planning?" Marion asked, perching her bottom to the left of his heart-shaped box of Valentine candies.

"Piece of cake."

"Very funny. Is she still in her meeting with Cherry Margaret?"

"Yup," he said.

"And when is it again?"

"The meeting?"

"The wedding."

"Oh. Three weeks."

"Three weeks. Sheesh. Wait. Isn't that the same weekend as sales conference?"

"You got it."

"That's weird." She extracted a chocolate from the box and stuck a thumbnail in the bottom. Inspected the interior and put it back. "So which comes first?"

"Um, sales conference. Sales conference is first. Then the wedding."

"I still can't believe you're getting married."

"Neither can I."

"Love will do that to a man," she said. "No explaining it. No figuring love." She leaned back, arching her chest, until she was obstructing his view of his computer screen.

"Um, Marion? Could you—"

"I can't believe I thought that Dawn and Fox were an item."

"Hoo-wee," he said. "How about that."

"I mean, what a scuzzbag. As if Dawn could be that dumb."

"I was thinking the same thing myself."

"You know he's cornered me on e-mail?"

Oscar stopped trying to look at his screen. "What?"

"E-mail. My e-mail address is on my stationery, and I had to send him the publicity plan for *Global Intrusion*. So now he's e-mailing me. Every day. Or night, according to the time on the headings."

"He is? What does he say?"

"Say? This is not speech, Oscar. It's drivel. Moaning, grunting. It's nauseating, I have to tell you. I've never seen anyone drool in cyberspace before."

"He's after you?"

"After me. Before me. He's there in my mailbox every time I log on. I have to get myself one of those V-chips."

"That's awful," he said. His mind was racing.

"Whatever." She picked up another chocolate and bit in delicately with her front teeth. "I see you're working on your seating chart." She pointed to the shelf beside his desk, where he'd deposited the shrapnel of his guest list atop the binder. "My sister did it the same way. Cut and paste, tape up the tables. Throw people together, keep the families apart. Does she—what's her name—have a big family?"

"Nope."

"That's a relief. And you don't, I know."

"True."

"Still, there are always the have-to-haves," she said. "Everyone who's ever had you to their wedding or baby shower or baptism. Summer shares, housewarmings, boat christenings."

"I'm not inviting those guys."

"That's it. Be selective. You don't want to end up with five hundred people on your list." She fussed with her hair, using his computer screen as a mirror. "Any publishing people?"

"Sure."

"Agents?"

"An agent, yes."

"Oh, goodie."

"Why don't you just ask, Marion?"

"Ask what?"

"You're invited."

"Am I? I was wondering. Not that I'd be heart-broken," she added. "Who else. Not Carl."

"Yup."

"Dawn? Did you tell Dawn?"

"Dawn knows."

"And in terms of single men—"

"I wouldn't know."

"Wouldn't you? I'd think you'd have to know."

"I could know."

"Maybe you could know sometime soon," she said. "Because funny things happen at weddings. People are seated together. People meet each other. People dance."

"Huh."

"And it all starts with them sitting next to each other. According to the seating chart."

"I take your point, Marion. I'll see what I can do."

"At a corner table, for instance."

"Don't push it."

Someone approached from down the hall as Marion bent to select another chocolate. It was Deborah, walking behind her, motioning theatrically—squaring an object in the air and shoving it off—that the cover was on its way. Oscar tried not to smile. Shooed her away.

"So where are you going on your honeymoon?" Marion asked him, straightening up and adjusting her bust.

"Oh, nowhere."

"Jamaica."

"No."

"Tuscany. Hawaii."

"No, no. I'm really not at liberty—"

"Is it an island? Tell me that much."

Oscar leaned back in his chair. "It's not."

"But it's a resort."

"Not really."

"A city, then."

"I'd call it a town."

"How long are you going for?" she asked. "You can tell me that."

"I can't say."

"You can't say how long your honeymoon's going to be?"

"I can't even say that we're going at all."

"You with your secrets. Let me give you a piece of advice, Oscar. Before your wedding." She threw down the wrapper from her chocolate. "You men think that secrets make you smarter. But they don't. They make you morons."

"That's true. You're right, Marion. I'll tell you." He took a chocolate himself. "Paris."

"I *knew* it," she said.

They traded grins, locked for a moment in the enjoyment of swapping secrets and munching chocolates, in the sense that comes with an upcoming wedding or the gaudy arrival of something great.

Cherry Margaret (born Sheryl Markowitz) was a best-selling romance writer who sauntered up from her estate in Atlanta once a year to shmooze the reps at sales conference and set out on a thirty-city tour to promote her latest airport favorite. Unlike Dawn, she seemed to have been mellowed by success, her voice having slowed, her pretentions having simmered to a sort of syrupy appreciation for the lowlier classes and loyal servants like Oscar. He had come to look forward to her annual arrival. This year, in addition, he needed her help.

She emerged from Dawn's office to greet him. "Whale, whale. *They-ah* he *is,*" she drawled. "Best-looking secretary in New York."

Rising from behind his desk, he stooped to receive a loud kiss on the cheek that left the impression he'd been hit by a pink-frosted doughnut.

"Let me see you." She held him by the hips and looked up. "I'll be darned if you don't got some sparkle to you."

"I do?"

"Sure do, sugar. I know my sparkle, and you've got it. You look like you're in love."

"Well, that's—"

"Anyhow, you look a sight better than the last time

I came up to this big old filthy apple to see y'all. You were fixing to keel over. Like a telephone pole with no connections." She slapped him on the leg. "You've been courting."

"A bit."

"You getting hitched, Oscar?"

"What?"

"Married."

"Oh. Yes. Yes, I am, actually."

"Attaboy!"

"I'm getting married," he repeated. And it was practically—potentially—true. He had someone, was currently without her, for the first time in his life. This was the shiver of freedom that he had longed for all along: the sense of everything ending, and finally beginning. "And how are you?" he asked.

"Pretty as a picture," she said.

The picture was rather hazy, the woman a fireball of static electricity in her sable coat and fur hat. The diamonds clustered beneath her ears were the size of bunches of grapes.

"You ready for sales conference?"

"I *adore* sales conference. You know that. That's where I get to spread my wings. Greet my troops."

"Well, the book's terrific, Cherry. Your best yet. Better than *Tango in Tennessee,* and that was my favorite."

"Don't tell me no *labs,* Oscar. You read my romances?"

"I read all Dawn's books."

"You *edit* all Dawn's books." She shook a finger up at him. "But that's our little secret."

"While we're discussing our little secrets," he said, stooping to guide her gently toward his desk, "could I ask you about something?"

"I'm all yours."

"You throw a lot of parties."

"All the *tahm*. Derby Day, General Lee's half birthday. I put together a gala for Arbor Day that made Woodstock look like a wake."

"With invitations and everything."

"Invitations *are* everything," she said. "Let me tell you."

He sat. "Please do."

When it comes time to decide on the folks worth admitting to the event (and that there's your first problem), there are rigorous laws (and here's your second) concerning how. Invitations are to be sent no sooner than six weeks before, returned no later than three weeks later, and created with nothing but the finest ingredients of flair. Cards may be lithographed or thermographed, letterpressed or engraved. Addressees ought to be hand-calligraphied, return addresses blind embossed. Write out street numbers and state abbreviations and spell out every darned detail of the day. Honor *honour* and favor *favour* with ceremonial British *u*'s. The bride gets mentioned before the groom; their parents get separate lines if they're divorced; children get sent separate invites if they're over thirteen. Mail your sweet self a sample to find out how long it takes to arrive—and be sure to include a note of encouragement, as the moment others are invited to the occasion, your attendance is required as well.

She slid on a pair of long pink gloves as she watched him finish his notes. "I've sent so many invitations to so many parties, I ought to write y'all a book on that."

"You already have," he pointed out. "That's the best part of *Moonlight*, when Dale sends the card to Isabella after he's been ordered off the plantation."

"Oooh, you *did* read it."

"And she reads it in the mill. Sobs into the newly spun cotton." He helped her into her coat. "Because she realizes that it wasn't his fault."

"Sure wasn't."

"And that she loves him."

"She does."

"That's when she aches. And aches. For the third time that page."

"Watch yourself, now."

"And he *throbbbs*. With three *b*'s."

"Leave me alone, you devil. I'm a writer, not a speller. That's what I have you for." His upside-down binder had caught her attention. "Is that the script you're fixing to use?"

He retrieved a sample card and held it before her. "That's it."

"Howdee do. And how many are you sending."

"Um, one."

Her lipsticked lips went taut.

"I know. There's an expl—"

"No, you don't know." Her fur coat bristled at him.

"A party for one person? It's just not *ðuhn.*"

"It's not what?"

"*Duhn.* Done," she pronounced flatly. For the moment she had forgotten her accent; and with the striking of that false note, her face seemed to change, losing its down-home peachiness. Her indignation had stripped her of all semisouthern charm. "No way," she snarled. She sounded as if she might be from Brooklyn.

"Oscar!" Dawn yelled from her office. "Oscar. Get in here, Oscar." She hit the intercom: *Bwahhh. Bwahhh. Bwahhh.* "Hell are you? Oscar."

"You're just going to have to invite more people," Cherry was saying.

"There'll be plenty of people. You'll see."

"I will? Am I invited?"

"Oscar!"

"A party without Cherry Margaret?" he said, grabbing his clipboard and leaving her with a smile. "It's just not *ðuhn.*"

He had escorted Dawn to the elevators, reminded her of her limo location, given her a fresh bottle of water and returned to his desk to phone the stationers and order one card, one envelope, one response card, and one response card envelope when Gordy called.

"Just missed her," said Oscar. "She's on her way home. Do you want me to leave a message? Or are you going to see her tonight. Or is it none of my business."

"Matter of fact, Big O, got other plans tonight." There was the sound of ice rattling in a glass. "Know what I mean?"

"I think I know what you mean." He pictured Gordy dead-drunk and sweating through an undershirt, tap-tapping out a dirty e-mail to Marion.

"So listen up." The unstoppering of a bottle. A galloping pour. "Just got a call from our man Kirk Connolly."

His face went stiff. "What did he have to say?"

"Got his new cover."

Oscar was holding the phone so hard that his hand hurt. He prepared for his grim victory: the breaking of the deal between Kirk Connolly and Dawn Books, the accompanying breakup of Gordy and Dawn. It had worked, he thought as he braced to endure the shouting. Soon to free himself of his life of civil slavery, he had successfully liberated his boss as well. What more could be expected of an excellent assistant? How else would he ever get hitched?

"So what does he think?"

A slurp. "What do you think he thinks?"

"I don't know." *I do know,* he thought. *I have known all along that this would work.*

"He loves it."

"What? He does? He loves the cover?"

"Loves it," said Gordy. "*Loves* its ass."

"I don't—really? Are you sure?"

"I'm sure, buddy. He said it's sort of a landscape doohickey. That right? Kind of a romance feel. So now the guy's all hyped up about his new start with his new publisher, hitting crossover markets he's never hit. A female readership. Double the sales. Thinks you're all geniuses."

Oscar let his head drop onto his desk with a bang. Phone to his ear. "I'm so pleased."

"Had my doubts," Gordy was saying. "Don't know how you people get anything done over there. But you do. *You* do, Big O. I know it's you pulling the strings. Jerking the chains. I know this business, and I'll tell you right now: it's run by the flunkies. By the nobodies you never see who amount to nothing," he crowed. "That's you."

E-mail was indisputable. E-mail, he thought, would be saved. Could be forwarded. And should serve as proof. This was his last stand, the final guerrilla tactic he came up with once left alone in the office. One more effort for her sake, and for his own. For good.

Marion's office was pasty with the smell of cosmetics. He pushed aside a cannister of lip gloss, hit the Power button, and took her chair. The screen fizzed on. The modem sirened into action. He remembered her password from the time he'd had to teach her Instant Messaging, scrolled past the memos he'd mailed her about sales conference over the course of the week. Before and after them was a heavy barrage of missives from gfox@foxagency.com as well as plenty from both foxygord and foxyguy@aol. It took him an hour to read through them, choose the lewdest, and steel his nerves. With the soft clack of a button, dawn@dawnbooks.com was besieged. He stretched his long arms above his head. Flunky feet on the desk. By the nobodies you never see, he thought, and let out his breath.

The Rehearsal

SHE SHOVED HER TRAY into the upright position and released herself into more of a slouch. After attending enough weddings, she thought, one moves from prim reverence through revulsion and finally comes to admire them with the depth of feeling they deserve. Humankind has invented no more poignant way to overspend money and energy. There is no grander festival of gestures and costumes, no more primal tribal sacrifice upon the altar of fate. She was as lucky as any bride to have gotten to see so many of them. She was coming full circle, now, flying back to New York for one more.

She untied, unbuttoned, and unfurled the invitation that Chris had forwarded to her hotel in Colorado a few days before. It was a many-splendored, gaudily embossed disaster, quite frankly, calligraphied on gilt-edged vellum and encased in an origami of rice paper together with various protective layers of lace. A confetti of dried flowers littered her lap and the carpeting at her feet. Enough sprigs and lumps of wood pulp were embedded in the heavy-stock envelope that she could have poured milk over the package and eaten it as an in-flight breakfast. The language, too, was hysterically overelaborate, going so far as to invite her (could they have done this for everyone?) by name. "The honourable presence of the estimable Lauren LaRose is hereupon and warmly requested"—and here she noticed, as she hadn't before, that the bride and the groom were never mentioned. Well, Oscar would be there, she thought as she stuffed it back in her bag. She would have the honor of his estimable presence one more time before she left.

She thought of putting on the plastic headphones and napping for an hour. She thought again of Oscar, and that opened her eyes. She worked her way back toward sleep by counting the cities she'd visited over the past few weeks. When that didn't do it, she labored to put them in alphabetical order. Boston, Bozeman, Champaign-Urbana. Denver. Nantucket. Roanoke.

But she'd forgotten Kansas (Lawrence was the origin of the flight) and lost interest in the exercise. She threw her pillow to the floor and watched time pass vacantly outside the window.

In two days she would return home—in triumph, her mother would say, thrilled to have someone enter through the screen door that had previously banged open only to let people out. She had held a fabulous job, toured the country, found fame. She had written for a living: what could be better than that? But she didn't write for a living; she had been kept from it by these stupid columns, trapped behind them like bars. A book would be different. A book would belong to her. She would work on a book in Idaho—ha, there was her reason to go home. She would take over the cabin out back by the cottonwoods, dust off her father's old mountain mahogany desk. The book, of course, would be about weddings; but rather than the way they're meant to be, she would write for once of the way they are. Of their heroic strain toward per-manence, their snatches at elegance, their glorious disarray. Of our struggle, like that of butterfly collec-tors, to pin down a day and admire it. Of the day's tendency, like a snowflake, to fly freely and uniquely awry. She was returning home in defeat, having cov-ered countless findings of someones only to lose someone of her own, or else let him lose her. At least she'd see him at the wedding tomorrow. The Book Wedding in the Big Apple. She could write the stupid thing now.

She gave up on dozing; she had the rural rest of her life for that. She pulled back down the tray table, took out her pen, and started to try to brainstorm for the book. Without notes it would be hard. It was all in her head, but packed too tightly to be pried out and onto the page. Notes were what she needed: bits of data, points of fact. She tried to drum up a notation, a squiggle of info to loosen herself up. This was how authors worked on books, she thought, taking heart. This was a good rehearsal, these fervent twitches on the brink of productivity.

In a minute she was asleep.

No question about it now: it had nothing to do with love. Dawn had to have gotten all the e-mails and read them, to have decided to move mechanically forward. Oscar's plan never stood a chance. All his efforts at antiassistance could have no influence on a woman who possessed not the slightest softness of heart. Interested as usual in the profits and losses, Dawn was gunning for the merger after all; marrying the man regardless in a mutually hostile takeover that couldn't be stopped. Oscar had been rooting for her humanity, it occurred to him, for years. He had been banking on a person behind the persona. And he'd lost.

The day before sales conference always had a whiff of the Apocalypse; but the lack of Dawn's detonation had sapped the day of its brewing gloom. In the calm Oscar sat and looked over the neatness and squareness of his life. Stapler, Scotch tape, and stamp pad were parked in a perfect line at one clean corner of his desk, his computer triangled at the other. The files in his deskside shelf were labeled with typed stickers, precisely half of them green-dotted, half of them red-. Above them a row of books was arranged according to date of publication. His telephone cord hung untangled. He had amounted to this: the tidy site of never-ending activity in the service of nothing and no one.

Tomorrow he would quit. He'd break it to Dawn during a lull in the lame festivities. He would leave the office this evening and simply never come back. By then he'd have served at sales conference, overseen the wedding, caught a last glimpse of Lauren, and could move on with no regrets. For over a decade he'd worked as Dawn's reluctant bodyguard; but she turned out to be invulnerable, as he'd learned by trying to poke at her emotions himself. And while he was capable of holding down a bad job—needless to say, after all these years—a pointless job was different. He could quit a pointless job without a second thought. And in twenty-four hours, he would.

So this was his final Friday morning. And suddenly afternoon. When Dawn slammed herself in her office to prepare her conference speech, he quietly worked the phone with scant hours to undo his plan. But unmaking the event turned out even harder than its concoction. First he called New Jersey to tell his father not to come; but the guy must have been swallowed in the roar of the

Nets game, the answering machine yet again (hadn't he fixed that?) out of tape. In Idaho there was no pick-up whatsoever, just the endless burring of what he pictured to be a wall-hung rotary phone. There was no point leaving a message at the magazine: Lauren was attending the event in any case, only with less of a prominent role than he'd hoped. He had taken his chance and squandered it. At five o'clock he called for Dawn's limo and sat back to watch the end of the day.

He had mentioned to Marion, irresistibly, that he was quitting, and word had spread rapidly from there. As a result, people stopped by in a parade of goodwill on their way out of the building. A round of hugs from the publicists on seven. The farewell blather of the legal assistant from twelve. An inordinately long speech on the importance of broadened horizons from a marketing executive who'd never spoken to him before. Carl looked aghast, shaking his hand with clammy fingers. Marion mushed him a kiss on the lips. They would see him tomorrow, in any case, at the conference; *at the wedding,* he thought glumly, waving them away with a smile. He gave his Rolodex one more spin; it wished him well, like a dolphin, with clicks. How little time it took, after all that, to plan his exit. How easily summarized and put away, these years.

He was rounding his desk to usher Dawn to the elevators when her voice boiled upward and shook like a kettle.

"Oscar. *Os*-car. *Oscaaar!*"

He found himself running toward her closed door. The shrillness of the call was promising. She was at her computer, he saw after turning the handle: another good sign. He cleared his face of all pleasant expectation as he came to a halt. "What's wrong."

"This fucking gizmo on the thing," she said. "It's broken."

He moved beside her and squatted to see the screen.

"I haven't been able to get my e-mail for two weeks. The goddamn hamster won't move."

"The mouse," he said. "Here. I think your screen's frozen."

"Who the hell froze my—"

"Hold on. Let's just shut down. Remember? These three buttons at once. There." The screen died and restarted with a zoom. "Now let's just try this again."

The cursor slid easily across the screen to open her e-mail. The downloading of messages took suspiciously—excitingly—long.

"A hundred and ten messages?" she shouted. "You screwed this up, Oscar. Click on something else. Exit. Fucking *backspace*, Oscar. Nobody can answer a hundred and ten goddamn messages. I've got a limo downstairs. Big day tomorrow. *You* can answer a hundred and ten messages, Oscar." She pushed back from the desk. "Tell them I'm online on another line and will get back to them."

"Maybe you should just look at these."

"You look at them." She was going for her coat.

"They may affect tomorrow."

She stalked back to the desk. Slitted her eyes. "Jesus, what *are* all those? I don't know anyone with the initials FWD."

"That means forward. They were forwarded."

Eventually he convinced her to sit. To open them one by one. After five or six she worked faster, letting her coat fall as she double-clicked and closed and opened, closed message number seventy-one and started to yell. Down poured her pens when she slapped aside the cup of them. To the floor banged her monitor, out the window a slew of curses. And then something solidified in her torn face: the desire—no, the deep need—to strike back. She looked to Oscar for assistance. He shrugged and gave her his idea. And for the next hour they practiced and polished the event, making lists of names and phone calls around the city as they rehearsed her revenge.

The end of winter comes to New York as a miracle. It was only mid-March, but already the slab of sky had cracked open to warm the stairways of brownstones, to flare in apartment windows and torch the dented bumpers of cabs. He left work as the sun descended. He decided against the subway in favor of a walk. He had told Dawn he quit, and the world hadn't ended. On the contrary, it shone pinkly as if newborn. He passed through midtown like a man on a stroll through a former neighborhood. He crossed Central Park amid the smell of the newness of trees, the struggle of baby grass as it shouldered its tiny widespread burden and hopefully, upwardly, pushed on.

The Day

THE DAY BEGAN MORE SMOOTHLY than he could have expected. The 105th floor was ready in plenty of time—chairs conference-style, handouts laser-printed, Dawn Books banner rightside-up—and the sales reps, hundreds strong, entered murmuring appreciatively at the view. Dawn appeared surprisingly tranquil, standing stage left and sifting through notes, as he watched her from behind the slide projector at the back of the room. She managed a polite hello to Cherry Margaret, rolling her eyes only when the woman, with a fling of her boa, moved away to take her seat. She remembered the name of the *Wonder of Wildflowers* author, nodded at Kirk Connolly as he swaggered past. She endured a soulful clasp from Tommy Gunn before wiping off her hand. The reps settled into the sea of chairs and shuffled the handouts. Waiting to address them, she wrenched her features into a welcoming smile.

These were true all-Americans, the unseen hitmakers: midwestern men in unimaginative ties and women from the southern cities come to judge on behalf of the book-buying millions who lurked in the vague nation outside New York. Regardless of any buzz generated on the high and tiny island of Manhattan, these were the people who took a book westward to the masses and made it big. For every Dawn there was a sales diva from Milwaukee who could make or break her by pitching her books to megastores across Wisconsin and starting a trend, or not. Each Dawn book passed through the ruddy hands of these reps on its way to store shelves—or to nowhere fast, if those hands let it drop. Dawn was familiar with, even fearful of, the power wielded by her audience, these dorks and broads from the middle of nowhere who determined, every season, her fate.

She looked back to Oscar and motioned for him to hit the lights. As she walked through the dimness to the spotlit podium, he adjusted the focus of the Dawn

Books logo being beamed above her head. Several hundred pens were clicked; notebooks opened with a sound like the luffing sails of an armada. Dawn strangled the neck of the microphone and began.

"Every book," she said—as the speech's editor, he could mouth along—"has a life of its own. A book is born. It lives. And it dies. Sometimes all in about a week and a half."

He clicked to a slide of the underselling Asian cookbook. There were chuckles.

"At the beginning of their lives, books aren't pretty. Just like people. They go to sleep for no reason, they can't digest things, they're covered in crap." Wary throat-clearings could be heard in a few of the rows. "But gradually they get stronger. More coordinated. They learn to speak, they learn to shave, they learn to drive themselves, and before you know it they're off on their own."

He cued the third slide: packed shelves in a bookstore. A rumble ran through the audience, fingers upraised toward the titles they'd represented to stores in the past. The headwaiter from the 106th floor pulled at Oscar's sleeve to let him know they were all set. Oscar nodded and shook him off. Slide four showed the front façade of the Dawn Books building.

"Here at Dawn Books, we have a responsibility," she resumed. "Our job is to care for these ugly fledglings and make them attractive enough to buy. We're an orphanage, people. We take 'em in, get 'em out. Books are born every day in the brains of authors, in the broken homes and filthy crack dens of artistic minds." She winced at the spotlight, dipped back into her notes. "They're dropped off at our door, dozens a week, with letters attached. *Take good care of my baby. Find a home for my precious.* And goddamn it, we do."

Amid tentative applause, Oscar looked to his right. Gordon Fox, in a tuxedo, had entered the back of the room. Right on time. Agents didn't generally attend sales conference; but he had been asked, the previous evening, to come early to the floor below his event. He crossed his arms over his bulging cummerbund and slipped into a shadow to watch.

"But the job doesn't stop there," Dawn was saying. "Because unfortunately, we've got to take care of authors as well. The know-nothing parents who gave birth to the things and handed them over. They follow their babies into our orphanage and need to be babied themselves."

Slide five was a montage of author photos. Cherry Margaret, seated beside the central aisle, touched a hankerchief to her forehead.

"Then we've got the baby-sitters showing up to wipe a few noses and demand fifteen percent."

Slide six: close-up of agent's contract. Oscar looked over to where Gordon was shifting in the dark.

"All of which makes our offices pretty crowded. Our job pretty damned hard. A real pain in the ISBN." A titter or two at that. "So why do we do it? One word for you, people. Love. Got that right. Books are orphans, I remind you: lonely and desperate and deserving a break. They may not be perfect, but they could all use a home. They may not be all that smart or good-looking, but they deserve to be loved. And that's where you come in."

Oscar flicked back to the Dawn Books logo as she wound down her introduction.

"Talk to our authors. They're all here somewhere. Get their autographs, get to know them. Then take their books out into the world. We trust you'll sell big to the chain stores, muscle into the independents, get us to the front of the window displays and cover-out on the shelves. Tommy Gunn has some psychopath fans in the Northwest; let's take advantage. Cherry Margaret is huge in the banjo-picking sticks; you can do better. This spring we're launching the new Kirk Connolly thriller"—eager whispers at that—"and if I don't see every God-fearing, Arab-hating, red-blooded and blood-thirsty American with a copy of that goddamn book on their lap by summer, you're all dead." She paused, having gone off track. She looked the length of the room at Oscar. *Love*, he mouthed. "Love," she said quickly, spreading her arms. "Love is the answer."

Gordy's laugh echoed strangely, unmicrophoned, throughout the room. When he looked up, the speaker's gaze was aimed directly at him.

"Yes, love," she repeated. "And speaking of love, *I* would love, at this point—before we move on to present you with our latest line of Dawn Books—to try something a little different. I'd love to hear from *you* people. If you'd love to say something. Anything. Opinions, insights. Fire away."

Oscar suppressed a grin, surveying the stunned reaction around the room.

"Why not? You people know books. I don't usually ask your opinion, so here goes. Speak your mind. Open your damned hearts. You there. In the seersucker. Any opinion on Dawn Books?"

A wan man toward the front looked behind twice before pointing to himself.

"Yeah, you. Speak up."

He took some time to gather his breath. "I would say," he put forth, "enough with the memoirs."

"That right?" Dawn moved back and forth on the stage, holding tight to her temper. "You think you can— Well, I asked."

"I'm only saying," he forged on, gaining confidence, "that we all have life stories. I have a life story, he has a life story, she has a life story." He pointed down his row at a burly fellow with rolled-up shirtsleeves and a woman with frizzy yellow hair like a tennis ball. "I just don't think we all have to publish them. Or that you do. Sooner or later terrible and wonderful things happen to all of us, I'm saying. But we don't all have to get royalties on them. That's all I'm saying."

"Got it. All right, then. So you've had enough of the memoir genre. I'll keep it in mind. Who else." She pivoted fiercely. "Other thoughts on our books. Or any other books. Who here's read a good book lately?"

"I'm into literary fiction," volunteered a young rep with a mustache. "I read *The Paucity of Bones*. That wasn't bad. Told from the point of view of a manatee. And *The Nourishment of Iambs*. Blind harpsichordist, ancient Bengal. Whole thing in verse."

Dawn coughed out a laugh. "You've got to be—"

"I read *The Withering of Sturgeon*. Prize winner in Germany. I'm just wondering if we should get in on that kind of thing. Literary fiction. The Something of Something."

"Worth a thought," she mustered into the mike. "Let's move on. Anyone out there had a *bad* literary experience lately? You there." She pointed with the microphone, like a talk show host, to a woman near the back who hadn't raised her hand. "Go ahead. Share the pain."

It was the associate publisher of Simon & Schuster: Gordy appeared to recognize her as Oscar did. Oscar watched him duck in place, hands in his tuxedo pockets, trying to make himself less likely to be noticed behind the rows and rows of chairs. Oscar reached toward the wall and switched the lights so that they came up in the back of the room. Hundreds of heads turned in a wave. Gordy appeared to shrivel in the glare. There were peeps of recognition here and there from his authors, drowned out by the general hush.

"Yes, I, well, did have a bad literary experience," the woman said clearly. Oscar had rehearsed her over the phone. "Something leapt out at me in a bookstore.

Really grabbed me. But it turned out to be pretty dumb."

"Dumb? That's too bad." Dawn let the mike droop empathetically. "Poor language? Or no story."

"No language. Definitely no story there. Just plain dumb. And these hideous hairs on his back."

Dawn met Gordy's wide eyes, amid mutterings, before hunting for someone else in the crowd. "How about you. Orange dress."

"Yeah, I got caught up in the same one," admitted the sub-rights assistant who had agreed to come forward when they found her the night before. She turned in her chair to watch Gordy as she spoke. "Kept me up, annoyingly, all night. Pure trash. Fat as can be. Thick, too: you know, *dense.*" She flashed him a smile. "But it petered out quickly."

"What was the problem?" asked Dawn.

She measured an inch in the air with her fingers. "Too short."

Gordon gave an audible groan and slunk toward the doors.

"Excuse me," Dawn boomed. "Waiter."

He stopped in his tracks. Revolved slowly to face the horde.

"Gordon," from the speakers on all walls. "Gordon Fox. Well, what do you know, ladies and gentlemen. The reviews are in. You've been panned."

He worked his hands. Moved his mouth. He looked, for all his seasoned ugliness, like he was thirteen years old.

"Unless anyone else wants to weigh in here with a similar experience. Open forum," she said. "Your show, people."

Several dozen hands were lifted around the room, representing a generous cross section of the publishing industry, albeit a particularly youthful and buxom sample. Oscar noted that, after a brief hesitation, Tommy Gunn sniffed and threw up his hand. But by that time, Gordon was gone.

Oscar looked back to Dawn through the forest of arms. From where he hunched beside the projector—stooping to the floor, now, to collect his leftover slides—he could see her pride, could feel traces, radiating out and over the rows from those small glittering eyes, of delight. She wanted nothing more. This was her story, this ongoing series of stand-alone moments, and he congratulated her on it from a pleasurable distance away.

"Which brings me to a scheduling announcement." She tapped on the mike. "Change of agenda. Sorry for the inconvenience, late notice, yadda yadda. We were originally planning, immediately following the book presentations, to have you all take the elevators one fl—"

She stopped short to stare straight ahead once again. Oscar turned in his crouch to witness Gordon's furious return—but before the doors was someone else entirely. Someone slimmer, more graceful, in a Boise State sweatshirt over jeans. The woman blinked at the big windows before moving cautiously toward the back row and then reversing into the beam of the projector, shielding her eyes. She must have recognized Oscar's squatting silhouette. She smiled, with a shrug of the shoulders, as she neared. There are moments like this: when all the long-shot odds fall, defeated, around the feet of the victors; when oceans of attitudes and conditions part miraculously to give way.

He dropped the slides as she reached him. He rose only halfway.

"Oscar?"

"Lauren."

"Are you okay? Why are you kneeling?"

He was floating, in fact, with a dizzy bird's-eye perspective that enabled him to see what to do.

"I want to ask you," he said.

"What are you—oh my God."

"I want to ask you to take a chance."

"You're not doing what I think you're doing. Are you doing what I think you're do— Are you doing it?"

"I want to ask you to marry me."

There was a churchly silence in the enormous room.

"In fact, I am," he said. "Asking you. To marry me."

"Now? Here?"

"Would you marry me, Lauren? In a couple minutes. Upstairs."

They faced each other—nearly eye-to-eye, blazing in the light of the projector—as if alone.

Over the course of my six and a half years of writing this column, I have witnessed underwater ceremonies and mountaintop betrothals, Sufi weddings and circus weddings, but never a surprise wedding; not until a recent Saturday evening spent a mile above Manhattan along with 500 other guests who had been invited minutes before. Any nuptials might have come as a surprise in this case, considering that in the six months since Oscar Campbell, 31, met his bride, the couple went out on precisely one date. Yet the mid-March occasion at the top of the World Trade Center was designed to astonish even the most experienced watcher of weddings.

The groom was dressed simply: navy blue blazer, Dawn Books tie. The bride wore a white gown she'd never seen before, given to her by the ex-boss of the groom in a clothes swap before the event. The service was conducted by Chris Lucas, a Ph.D. candidate in theology, and consisted of vows written and edited by Oscar and the reading of a Shakespearean sonnet by his friend Carl Appelfeld. The groom had inherited the bride's ring from his employer a few hours before; and when the minister-in-training gave the go-ahead, it fit.

Following the ceremony was a live performance of the couple's song, "Love Can Bite Me," by platinum-selling artist (and author of the forthcoming autobiography *I Suck*) Tommy Gunn. Around the tables of the skytop restaurant, decorated with avalanches of lilies of the valley, guests dined on Idaho steaks and pota- toes. Dessert arrived as a hail of *cro- quembouche*, tossed at the revelers by a French dessert chef with a tireless arm and lousy aim.

By the time the meal had been cleared and Mr. Gunn had smashed his second electric guitar, the dance floor was crowded all the way to the wall-sized windows. The minister box-stepped with Cherry Margaret, best-selling author of such romances as *Valentine in Virginia*. Book publicist Marion Hawes was boosted onstage to gyrate alongside Mr. Gunn. Dawn Davis, president and publisher of Dawn Books, looked sporty in a baggy Boise State sweatshirt as she took a spin in the arms of blockbuster writer Kirk Connolly. And as the groom's father and the bride's mother shared a digni- fied waltz, the newlyweds performed a cavorting limbo-cum-rhumba that had obviously been practiced, if not per- fected, before.

"Ever since he was little — young, I should say — Oscar's been a bit of a wall- flower," said his father, Wade, a slim man with his son's impressive height and shy smile. "He's always been content to help out around the house, and pleased to see others do well. He's a bookworm, and bookworms get in the habit of living off the adventures of other characters. So it's nice to see him heading out on an adventure of his own."

Bridget LaRose was just as happy for her daughter. "All her life she's been pursued by men, but none of them was quite right. They were all . . . *small* men," she recalled. "Smaller than life." She gazed at the groom as he piggybacked his wife toward the dessert table. "Lauren always wanted someone larger than life. Someone big enough to sweep her off her feet."

As it happens, the two have swept each other further away than that: to Paris, Idaho, the farmy town near the southeast corner of the state where the bride was born. She is writing a book about weddings, with the help of the notes Oscar amassed in the course of plotting this one. He is enjoying a clean start in a place that doesn't dwarf him. And this column will continue next issue and in the future, only written from now on by somebody else.

For I was the bride, in case you hadn't guessed. I hadn't. That was my wedding. He is my husband. These are our boxed belongings, arriving ceaselessly by Idaho post—a mountain of them already in the potting shed—and always from the same store registry across the country. I wonder whether we'll ever use three dozen soup bowls. Then I look up at Oscar and out over our wheat field and, closing my eyes as if to hold in the rest of our life, say: yes.